PROMISES

THE KINGS OF GUARDIAN, BOOK 14

KRIS MICHAELS

Copyright © 2020 by Kris Michaels

All rights reserved. No part of this book may be reproduced or transmitted in any form or by any means, electronic or mechanical, including photocopying, recording, or by any information storage and retrieval system without the written permission of the author, except where permitted by law.

If you are reading this book and did not purchase it, then you are reading an illegal pirated copy. Make sure that you are only reading a copy that has been officially released by the author.

This book is a work of fiction. Names, characters, places, and incidents either are products of the author's imagination or are used fictitiously. Any resemblance to actual persons, living or dead, events, or locales is entirely coincidental.

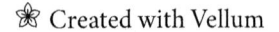

❦ Created with Vellum

THE KINGS OF GUARDIAN FAMILY TREE

Patriarch & Matriarch of the Marshall-King Family:

Frank Marshall is the widowed father of Victoria and Keelee Marshall. Amanda King is the widowed mother of Joseph, Justin, Jasmine, Jade, Jason, Jewell, Jared and Jacob King. She and Frank are now married to each other. She is now Amanda King-Marshall.

Marshall & King Children

Jacob (Skipper) King is married to Victoria (Marshall) King. They have four sons, Talon, Trace, Tanner, and the baby, Tristan.

Joseph King is married to Ember (Harris) King. They have one son, Blake King.

Doctor Adam Cassidy is married to Keelee (Marshall) Cassidy. They have one daughter, Elizabeth (Lizzy) Cassidy.

Jason King is married to Faith (Collins) King. They have two sons, Reece and Royce King.

Jared King is married to Christian (Koehler) King. They have one son, Marcus.

Jasmine (Jazz) King is married to Chad Nelson. They have one daughter, Chloe Nelson.

Jewell King is married to Zane Reynolds.

Jade King is married to Nicolas (Nic) DeMarco.

Justin King is married to Danielle (Dani Grant) King.

Drake (Simmons) Marshall, is married to Doctor Jillian (Law) Marshall.

Dixon (Simmons) Marshall is married to Joy (Moriah) Marshall.

Mike White Cloud (Chief) is married to Tatyana (Taty) Petrov.

The founder of "Guardian" and boss of most of the people mentioned above:

Gabriel Alexander (David Xavier) is married to

Anna. They have four children, Gabrielle (Gabrielle Jacqueline), the oldest daughter, twin sons Deacon and Ronan (David Ronan), and Charlotte (Charlotte Jacqueline).

Happy Reading!

Kris

CHAPTER 1

"I hate fucking parties."

Jacob King choked on his bourbon at his brother Joseph's words. Joseph gave him a side-eyed glare, but damn it, the guy was hilarious. When he could suck air, he replied. "You hate everything."

Joseph rolled his eyes. "Not true."

Pushing Joseph's buttons probably wasn't smart, but the bourbon was going down easy tonight which, according to Tori, always made him a bit stupid. He grinned. *Stupid was fun, especially around his brothers.* He pointed at his brother with the same hand that held his glass of bourbon. "Name one thing."

"Ember and Blake." Joseph rasped his wife and

son's names. A rare smile appeared. "That's two." A satisfied sneer crossed Joseph's face.

Jacob shook his head. "That's a given, and it wasn't what——"

"Miss Amanda," Dixon piped up.

"Frank," Drake added.

"Knives." Chief sniggered the word and lifted his damn snifter of cognac.

"Fighting." Adam leaned back in his chair and let a shit-eating grin spread across his face.

"Family and, believe it or not, I think that even includes you, Jacob," Justin added as he sat down in the plush back room of a club in Charlottesville, Virginia.

Jacob straightened. "Hey——"

"That godforsaken desert," Christian said and nudged his husband, Jared, who nodded and added, "Torturing the people who go through the training courses in that godforsaken desert."

Maliki Blue laughed and grabbed the bottle of bourbon that was behind him. "That's the truth, but I'll admit I know one thing this man is madly happy about that none of the rest of you do." He poured the men gathered another round except for Chief and Jason. Jason had his ever-present soda and Mike drank that damned frou-frou cognac that he'd taken a shine to when he was undercover as David Xavier.

The door opened, and Zane Reynolds ushered in Nic DeMarco and Chad Nelson. "*Son of a bitch!* Do you get that *everywhere* you go?" Zane shut the door behind him and motioned to Chad, the rumpled country singer. "The high-class clientele out front mauled Chad. I could only imagine what would happen if he walked through a honky-tonk."

"It's part of the job." Chad tugged on his shirt and tried to see the back. "Did she rip it?"

"No, but it was a close call. Man, those fans need rabies *and* distemper shots." Nic ambled over to the bar and grabbed three tumblers.

"I rarely enter through the front doors. Jazz arranges for us to enter and exit through other entrances. She keeps us out of the public eye and safe." Chad tugged on the sleeves of his shirt and took an empty tumbler from Nic. They dropped into chairs and held out their glasses. "What did we miss?"

Jacob answered, "About four rounds of great bourbon and Joseph declaring he hates parties."

Zane chuckled. "What about the one in Belfast?"

Joseph barked out a laugh. "That wasn't a party,

that was a melee, and it was one of the best times I've ever had."

"Your definition of a good time needs work," Jason chuckled and turned back to Maliki. "You were going to say something?"

"Not if he values his life, he wasn't." Joseph leveled a stare at Mal.

"Dude, lose the grump, I wouldn't actually say anything to them unless you brought it up first." Maliki finished the bottle and headed to the bar to get another one.

"Brought what up?" Jacob turned to stare at his oldest brother.

A slow smile spread across Joseph's face. Jacob had seen that pride before. Hell, he saw it in the mirror every time he thought about his boys. Jacob blinked. Could Joseph and Ember be… "No."

Joseph nodded.

"No way!" Justin hooted.

"Yeah, we're pregnant." Joseph's smile lit the room up.

"Holy hell! Congratulations." Jacob gave his brother a bear hug and then got the fuck out of the way as the rest of the men took their turns congratulating the oldest King.

Joseph flipped off his best friend. "You were

told not to mention it tonight, asshole. This weekend is about you and Poet."

"It still is! There is more than enough happiness to go around. Just don't let our mothers find out about the baby or they will plan the world's largest baby shower." Mal pulled a box of Cuban cigars from behind the bar. "Besides, now I can smoke one of these bad boys."

Joseph narrowed his eyes and grabbed a Cohiba Siglo VI. "Damn straight, and as this is *your* bachelor party, shouldn't we be doing some drinking and smoking anyway?"

Jason took a cigar and smiled. Jacob loved to see his brother be able to partake in the camaraderie. His addictions didn't extend to smoking, so watching him get involved in the festivities was a damn good experience. Jason clipped the end and lit up before he spoke, "Yes, but now we are celebrating both occasions."

"Besides, it's much more fun to irritate you. Mal just laughs the shit off," Drake said and then clinked his glass with Dixon.

Joseph slowly turned his attention to Drake. "Boy, you better back up, or we'll talk about a certain cabin that no longer exists."

Jacob laughed along with everyone else as

Drake's face flamed. "I offered to pay for the damage." The sullen, muttered reply ignited another round of laughter.

"Where are you and Poet going for a honeymoon?" Nic's question settled the commotion to a low roar, although Dixon and Drake continued to mutter between themselves while glancing at Joseph. *Well now, that could be of interest. Get those two plotting together and more than a mere cabin could blow up.*

Jacob tuned back into the conversation as Mal replied, "An all-inclusive resort on Aruba. Beachfront, all the alcohol, food, sun, and surf we can stand for two weeks." Maliki raised a glass and nodded to Joseph. "His idea."

Joseph's head whipped around. "What? So not my fucking idea!"

"Yes, it was. All you could do was go on about having Ember to yourself for two weeks in Aruba. Sounded damn good, so I looked into it. Should be heaven."

Joseph rolled his eyes. "Just don't stop by, if you know what I mean."

"No worries, I'll have better things to do than find your grumpy ass."

"Aruba for two weeks. Damn, that sounds like

heaven, especially after all these snowstorms." Justin leaned back. "Coldest winter in the last three decades. I hate the snow sometimes."

"Aruba, isn't that another desert?" Christian lifted his glass. "The man loves the desert."

"But it is a tropical desert island with beautiful beaches, and it's fucking *warm*." Zane lifted his glass and downed it in one go. "I could deal with two weeks laying on the beach."

Jacob couldn't help laughing at the glare Joseph sent Zane's way. This shit was getting fun. "I'm due vacation time. Aruba sounds fucking phenomenal."

Joseph slowly turned his head toward him. "Do not start."

"What?" Jacob smacked an innocent expression on his face. "Like you own the fucking island?"

"Last time I checked he didn't, but that mansion he lives in could be the Governor's Palace." Justin shrugged. "It has, what, ten bedrooms?"

"Yeah, we got lost when we stayed there last year." Chad nodded. "Ten bedrooms, thirteen bathrooms, a pool the size of a small lake, plus a beachside kitchen. That place is lit."

"I think Marcus would love the beach." Jared glanced at his husband and smiled.

"Oh, man, that would be amazing. It has been so damn cold here." Christian leaned into Jared.

Jason shook his head. "Unfortunately, I'm too busy. Mopping up the fallout from the New York situation."

"Thank God, that's all I'd need, the entire family showing up on my doorstep." Joseph gave an exaggerated shiver, tossed back the rest of his bourbon, and held out his glass toward Maliki. "I need another. I have to wear a fucking tux tomorrow."

"We know, that's why we're here. Well, that and wishing you well, Mal." Jacob lifted his glass.

"The people in this room and your spouses are the only ones Poet and I know, so we are very grateful you came. Our mothers have lost it. I swear it upset them when we capped the invitations. They had a list of over six hundred. Six hundred! Poet's mother wanted to invite relatives she's never met. And my mom? God, everyone she ever met would have an invitation. I'm so looking forward to Aruba. But in deference to our jobs and the people we wanted to invite, they agreed to a drastically smaller ceremony. Thank God." He glanced at his watch. "We leave the reception in twenty-three hours." Mal poured another drink. "To sanity, may it reign forever."

"To sanity." The toast echoed around the room as the door opened and platters of food arrived.

The aroma brought a rumble of dissatisfaction from his stomach. Jacob was so hungry his gut was pretty damn sure his throat had been slit. He hadn't eaten all day and his stomach was empty… well, minus the deluge of alcohol. He made his way to the first platter that hit the table. *Oh, hell yeah. Decent food.* He picked up a plate and piled on the eats. Two pieces for his plate, one for his mouth. *Fuck yeah, excellent food.*

"Hey, Skipper."

Stopping for a moment, Jacob glanced around with his fork halfway to his mouth before he shoved the flakey cheese puff in. "What are you two up to?" He said the words around his food.

"Want to have some fun?" Drake took a drink of his bourbon.

Uh, hell yeah! "Absolutely. But if it involves moving from this food, it will have to wait."

"You don't know what it is yet." Dixon laughed and grabbed a fancy sandwich from one of the trays next to them.

"Fuck, that looks good. Okay, then tell me what

you have in mind." Jacob pulled two of the small-ass sandwiches off the tray and plopped one on his plate. He took a bite of the other and waited for one of the Wonder Twins to speak.

Drake lifted an eyebrow. "Well, it involves pranking Joseph."

Jacob shrugged. "I'm in." He devoured the other half of the sandwich in one bite.

Dixon took a sip of his bourbon. "Got to be honest with you, Skipper. We're considering taking it to the next level. This could get you killed."

"Nah, he won't kill me." Jacob swallowed and glanced at his brother who was speaking to Mike and Maliki. He turned back and laughed, "At least I don't *think* he would. What are we doing? Switching out his tux?"

Drake shook his head. "Something so much better."

Jacob stopped eating and smiled. "Have I told you how much I miss your devious asses?"

"Not lately, but we know." Dixon turned his back to Joseph and company. "It will take some coordination."

Jacob picked up his drink. "With whom?"

"Everyone here, Frank and Gabriel, maybe a

few more." Drake murmured the words. "But it will be worth it."

He smiled and grabbed two more sandwiches, making sure Joseph was still across the room. "All right. Fill me in."

Ten minutes later, Jacob drew a deep breath. "You're right. He's going to kill us."

"You. Not us." Dixon pointed at him.

"No, if people are dying, it will be an equal opportunity murder scene. I'll rat you out the first chance I get." He downed the rest of the alcohol in his glass. "All right. Operation Get Maliki and Joseph Shit-Faced is a go."

Drake snickered, "Skipper, you have balls the size of Texas."

"Yeah. Hopefully, my brother doesn't cut them off, roast them, and force-feed them to me."

"It's all in fun, right?" Dixon shrugged. "We need this. All of us."

Jacob laughed and lowered his voice. "And the fact that it will irritate the fuck out of Joseph is just the cherry on the top, right?"

"More like the explosion on the top," Dixon and Drake said in unison.

Jacob blinked and shook his head. "Yeah, don't do that again. Wait until I have more liquor."

CHAPTER 2

P oet and Maliki's Wedding Day

Ember opened the bedroom door and padded out to the living area of the luxury suite Joseph had rented. She stared at the prone form of the man she loved and shook her head. Getting just the right angle, she took a picture before opening the group text between her and the Crazy Coven, as they called themselves.

>EMBER: Is mine the only one in this condition?

. . .

She attached the picture and hit send.

Joseph snored lightly, and she eyed him as she watched bubbles pop up on her screen. Shirt rucked up to his armpits, sprawled out on his back, one leg more off the couch than on with one shoe and sock off, one shoe and sock on. His hair stuck up in angles that the best sculpting wax couldn't achieve.

> *TORI: Nope.*

A picture of Jacob holding his head at a small table while his boys ate breakfast hit the group thread.

>*TORI: I ordered him sunny-side-up eggs, bacon, sausage, and corn beef hash, and told the boys they needed to spend time with their dad this morning. Strangely, he hasn't eaten a thing.*

Ember snorted. She absolutely loved Tori. The woman kept her man in line.

>*JASMINE: Chad and his new manager are heading*

to D.C. for a meeting with his lawyer. He said he nursed one drink all night. Did Jacob say anything about Aruba?

>JADE: Nic is in the shower. I think he might die in there. What the hell did they do last night? What about Aruba?

>FAITH: Jason took the boys to the airport to meet Amanda and Frank. He said something about going to Aruba.

Ember narrowed her eyes and turned her head slowly. "Joey, what did you do?"

Her husband's eye opened slightly. "Shhhh. Dying."

The croaking words substantiated the fact that her husband was in fact suffering. *Poor Joey.* "I've never heard of anyone dying from a hangover."

"Wait for it." His eye closed again. She shook her head and glanced back down at her phone.

> JOY: Mine's in a coma. Damn men can't hold their liquor. I want Starbucks. Hit me with room numbers and your orders.

A flurry of orders pinged on the thread, and Ember added hers.

>JASMINE: *Everyone come to mine. Joy, do you need help with the orders?*

>DANI: *I'll help. Meet you in the lobby. Justin is down in the gym. Probably in the sauna dying.*

> TATY: *Mike has one eye open. He's green.*

>KEELEE: *Okay if I bring Lizzy? Adam is dry heaving.*

>TORI: *Bring her to our suite, Jacob/Talon can watch her while we plot our revenge.*

>JILLIAN: *No revenge plotting needed. I've got the scoop. Meet you in ten minutes.*

>JADE: *It's a date. Jazz, order us breakfast?*

>JASMINE: *Got it. Hurry up.*

>JEWELL: *Just woke up to find my husband passed*

out in the hall between the bathroom and the bedroom. WTF did they do last night?

>JADE: *They got stupid drunk. Make sure he's breathing and come to Jazz's.*

> JEWELL: *The way he's snoring, I'm pretty sure he's breathing.*

A picture of Zane on his stomach, no shirt and no shoes or socks on the floor in the hall accompanied the text.

Ember chuckled and headed back into the bedroom to change for an impromptu breakfast party in Jasmine's room. Not more than five minutes later she was out of the bedroom again.

"Where're you going?" Joseph's craggy voice stopped her as she walked past him.

"Jasmine's room for breakfast. Unless you'd rather I ordered something and eat it here? I'm in the mood for a big breakfast. Bacon, cheese grits, sunny-side-up eggs with runny yolks."

Joseph groaned and brought both hands to his face, covering it. "You don't love me anymore." The pitiful whine made her laugh.

"Oh, you poor, poor man. That's not true. I love

you more than ever. I put two Tylenol on the counter in the bathroom. I'll be back. You have six hours before you need to meet Mal at the venue. I suggest you drink a lot of water."

"I hate him."

"You don't, he's your best friend." Ember grabbed her purse and dropped her phone into it. "I'll be back in an hour or so."

The mumble Joey gave could have been anything.

"Love you, too!" Ember smiled as she said the words a bit too loud and let the hotel door shut with a resounding thud.

She took a right at the end of the hall and knocked on Jasmine's door. The Kings had taken over all the suites at the Charlottesville hotel.

"Hey!" Jasmine opened the door for her and then flipped the privacy bar so the door would remain open. "How bad is he?"

"Alive enough to whine. He's just lucky Blake is with Amanda and Frank. I could just imagine Blake doing a leaping pin move on Joey this morning. I hope he's able to hold his head up by the time the bride walks down the aisle."

"No doubt. Chad will be back in time to get ready for the wedding."

"It was so nice of him to agree to sing."

"He likes the smaller crowds, but he wants this to be about Mal and Poet. We'll enter right before the groomsmen and groom take their places. He's playing the bridal procession on his guitar and singing one song, then, as soon as the bride and groom leave the sanctuary, we will dart out the side door to a waiting limo and head to Chad's mom's to pick up Chloe."

"It's such a shame that you can't enjoy the reception."

"I guess, but you learn to deal with it." Jasmine sat down on one of the long leather couches. "So, what's up with Aruba? Chad said something about maybe going there?"

"When?"

"Knock, knock." Faith pushed the door open and sauntered in. Of all the sisters-in-law, Faith was the quietest and the sweetest.

"Hey! Come on in." Jazz waved at the seats. "Frank and Amanda land okay?"

"They did. Jason is taking everyone to breakfast before they go back and get Gabriel and Anna." Faith yawned and sighed. "Man, I don't know what it is about this weather that makes me so dang tired."

"The lack of sunshine is my go-to answer." Ember understood being tired—man, did she ever. "Where are Gabriel and Anna staying?"

"What? I thought Gabriel and Anna were in D.C.?" Jade asked as she and Jewell walked in unannounced. Jade plopped down on the floor beside Jasmine, and Jewell curled up in the couch's corner.

"Guess they came to visit with Frank and Amanda while they were this close." Faith shrugged. "Are we going to Aruba?"

Jade dropped her head back. "Fuck, I wish. It's freaking cold as a witch's tit in a brass bra out there."

Jewell added a yawned, "In December."

"Anyone home?" Keelee and Tori strolled into the suite. Ember waved at Keelee and patted the chair cushion next to her. Keelee dropped into the seat with her and Tori took a seat across from them. "Coffee?" Tori glanced around.

"Here." Joy carried an oval busboy's tray with all the coffees balanced on it. Dani and Jillian trailed her. "There is one normal-ass coffee on that tray. Anyone touches it and they die." Joy's words stopped everyone's dive to the tray.

"You should work on your manners, yes?" Taty

came into the room and laughed at everyone's expression. "See? They are like scared rabbits. She probably wouldn't kill you."

"Yes, I would." Joy grabbed a cup and moved to the far corner of the seating area and sat down on the floor.

Ember watched as Jade and Jewell dove into the tray, looking for their drinks. "Who the fuck ordered orange herbal tea?" All eyes lifted at Jade's question.

"That would be me," Ember answered.

A squeal that could have awakened the dead reverberated through the room. They mauled her with hugs and congratulations. "When are you due?"

"Six months." Ember pushed her hair away from her face. "But look, this weekend isn't about me, it's about Poet and Mal."

"More like Poet and Mal's moms, from what Jason told me." Faith snorted and then looked up, her eyes wide. "Oh, poo, I said that in my big person voice, didn't I?"

"Oh, my god, that was awesome!" Jillian laughed. "I didn't know you had *any* snark in you!"

Faith's face flushed. "I have plenty of snark, I just rarely *say* what I'm thinking."

"Quiet ones." Joy nudged Taty, who'd sat down beside her. "Dangerous."

"Pot, meet kettle," Taty threw back at her.

Joy rolled her eyes and took a long drink of her coffee. She snapped her fingers after she finished. "Aruba. Speak."

Jillian jerked her attention to Joy. "Rude much? We've talked about this, Joy. People don't respond well to commands."

Joy sighed. She put her coffee down and jumped up to her knees, putting her hands together in supplication. "Please, Jillian, tell us what you know about Aruba. Like, that would totally be awesome!" The valley girl accent was dead on and sent everyone into fits of laughter.

"Fine, since you asked so nicely, Drake--"

"Wait, where's the food?" Jade interrupted.

Ember tossed a pillow at her. "Room service takes a while, now hush."

"Bossy. Just like Joseph," Jade muttered and leaned back. "Please, by all means, gossip is *so* much more important than my stomach."

"Agreed," Taty snarked.

Jade rolled her eyes and muttered something about being hungry. Jillian disregarded Jade and continued, "Anyway, Drake and Dixon hatched a plan with Jacob last night."

"Oh, shit. How much is *this* going to cost me?" Tori hung her head. Her long blonde ponytail swished over her shoulder.

"I'm not sure, but they got Joseph drunk enough that he invited everyone to Aruba for two weeks. The bosses are meeting today to clear everyone's schedules. I think Gabriel is renting out a house just down from Joseph's so there is room for everyone."

Joy snorted. "That explains it."

"Say what?" Jasmine asked.

Joy shrugged. "Text last night at about one-thirty. Dixon asked if he had a swimming suit."

"Does he?" Jade leaned forward so she could see Joy.

"Beats the fuck out of me." Joy sighed. "I'm not into this shit."

"Yeah, but you and Dixon could do other things and not spend too much time with the family." Jillian leaned back and kicked her legs out. "I'm going. I'm tired of being frozen."

"What about Ember?" Tori pointed at her.

Ember blinked and looked from woman to woman. "What about me?"

"Isn't this your vacation we're piling on top of?" Tori cocked an eyebrow.

"Yeah, but I don't care. We'll have a great time. Seriously, ten bedrooms. Everyone can do what they want during the day and we'll have a big dinner together. Not a problem." Actually, she kind of loved the idea. Dealing with Joey when he figured out his two weeks of alone time would not happen, on the other hand... "I really hope he remembers inviting everyone." She said the words more to herself than anyone else.

A snort came from the corner of the room. "Holy shit. Okay, I'm in."

Dani leaned over to see Joy. "Why the sudden change of heart?"

Joy shrugged. "I want to see him explode." She made an explosion with her hands to emphasize her point.

A knock at the door interrupted the conversation. Jazz hurried to the door, opening it for several wheeled carts of room service. Jasmine hurried to sign the bill while Jade lifted lids.

"Is this going to be too much for you?" Keelee asked in a whisper.

Ember leaned over and replied softly, "No. We have a staff at the house. I'll call down today and inform them of the change and ask them to get some temporary help. It won't be a problem."

"I mean with you expecting." Keelee bumped their shoulders together. Ember had told Keelee as soon as she and Joseph had told Amanda and Frank. She still talked to her best friend a couple times a day even though several states separated them.

"No, actually, I've had no morning sickness with this one. If I wasn't late, I wouldn't have suspected."

"Then it's a girl." Keelee smiled at her.

"You can't know that." Ember shook her head.

"I'm right." Keelee shrugged. "I knew Tori was having a boy each time and I knew I was having a girl."

"She also guessed about Chloe." Jasmine handed them each a plate.

"And about Royce," Faith added from the other side of the food-laden tables.

"This baby shit isn't catchy, is it?" Jade's eyes grew large. "I'm not okay with that."

"No, Jade, we've had this talk. You know how babies are made." Jewell scooped up a chocolate-covered donut. "Yummy. Food of the gods."

"How are you not the size of a barn?" Dani stared at Jewell as she demolished the sugar bomb.

"High metabolism." Jewell said the words around a massive bite of chocolate-covered goodness.

Jasmine asked, "So, we're all going to Aruba? When?"

Jillian gave a shrug. "Drake said he and Dixon would fly everyone. Except for Ember and Joseph, no one has packed for a tropical vacation."

Ember snorted. She had packed very little. The plan was to be naked and alone most of the time, but she had clothes at the house.

"I heard that." Tori laughed at her. "Did you pack anything besides lingerie? Amanda and Frank were watching Blake, right?"

Ember felt her face flame. "I have clothes at the house in Aruba, but I'm not saying we won't disappear after dinner."

The laughter that filled the room also filled her heart. She loved these women. Her Crazy Coven.

"So, have you picked out the next B name?" Jade asked as she licked her finger after drizzling honey onto an English muffin.

"We have. Brooke for a girl and Barrett for a boy."

"That's cool 'cause you need to take the cousins into account," Jewell said between bites.

Dani nodded. "We met Brianna a couple of years ago. She's sweet."

"Cousins? You mean the ones in Hope City?" Faith took a sip of her coffee.

"Yep. Let's see, Brock, Brianna, Brody, Bekki, and Blay," Jade rattled them off in order.

Ember nodded. "We discounted those names immediately. Didn't want to duplicate."

"When will you find out if you're having a boy or a girl?" Taty asked.

"Usually between the eighteenth and twenty-first week, so it would push it to find out before Christmas."

"But you're going to push it, right?" Tori asked.

Ember smiled. "Oh, yeah. Definitely."

"Wait. Has anyone seen Poet yet this morning?" Faith turned and looked around the room.

Jasmine answered, "She has a day planned with her maid of honor. They are doing a spa day, then makeup and hair."

"I bet her mother flipped out when she said there would only be a maid of honor." Ember chuckled. "Poor Poet was at The Rose training while the mothers were setting this monster up.

She was adamant, though. A best man and a maid of honor, and she was picking her own bridal gown. Other than that, she gave the mothers carte blanche until they heard about the people that the moms wanted to invite, then they screwed that down, too."

"Man, maybe I should have done that." Jade took a bite of her muffin.

"What?" Faith asked.

"Had my mom plan the wedding. It would have been easier, that's for sure." Jade shrugged.

"It would have saved me from seeing that puke green monstrosity you called a dress." Jasmine shuddered and rubbed her arms.

"Puke green?" Joy chuckled. "Knew you had shit taste."

Jade lifted her middle finger. "Har, har, har, and fuck you. I messed up the color number. It worked out. The wedding went off without a hitch."

"Except your fiancé went missing," Faith giggled. "And the ring thing."

Jade nodded her head. "Well, there was that."

Keelee sighed, "We've had every type of wedding between us, haven't we? A Tuscan Villa for Dani and Justin. Beachside for Ember and Joey."

Jasmine pointed across the room. "And Jewell and Zane."

"Actually, we got married on a boat," Jewell reminded her. "We had the reception at your house." She glanced at Ember and lifted another donut. "Best dessert bar ever."

Ember snorted. "That was all Justin and Dani."

"Your boat was beach-adjacent," Keelee amended.

"True," Jasmine laughed. "Chad and I got married in a small chapel in his hometown. Keelee and Adam tied the knot in a church in South Dakota. The same one Jade got married in."

"Mike and I married in Switzerland. Where we met." Taty smiled and blushed.

"That is so romantic." Tori smiled. "A judge married Jacob and me, and we consummated the marriage on my office floor." There was a moment of silence before every woman in the room cracked up laughing. "Hey, we didn't know if he'd be coming back. It was... so *not* romantic. But damn, it was hot." Tori's laughter joined everyone else's.

Jillian raised her hand before she spoke. "I hijacked Joy's wedding day."

"Like those two men would get married on

different days." Joy glanced at Faith. "Where did you get married?"

"Well, originally, we planned to get married in Vegas."

"Except for the Russian interruption." Tori nodded.

Faith shrugged. "So, we said our 'I do's in South Dakota. Probably the same Justice of the Peace that married the two of you." She pointed to Joy and Jillian.

"Who else here is planning on having children?" Tori sipped her coffee before she added, "I've been pulling the lion's share of this grandchild bearing thing. Time for you ladies to get into the groove."

"I want a kid." Joy's words snapped every head in her direction and silenced all conversation. "What?" She narrowed her eyes and then shrugged with a muttered, "Whatever."

"No! I think it's wonderful that you want a baby!" Tori spoke in a hurry, trying to eliminate the silence. "You'd make a fierce mom."

"That's the truth. No one would fuck with your kids, that's for sure." Jade nodded. "You go for it. I'd like to see Dixon as a dad. I think between the two of you you'd raise some awesome kids."

"What about you, Taty?" Jillian asked.

Taty blushed an adorable color of pink. "Mike and I don't use protection. If it happens, it happens, but so far, no luck. So we wait."

"I want a couple of kids someday," Dani added. "Soon, but there are things Justin and I want to do before we have children."

"Base jumping off of Mount Everest. Talk about kick-ass parents." Jade widened her eyes. "You two do you, you know what I mean?"

Jewell nodded and added, "I'm not against kids. Just not sure I understand their programming."

"They don't have any," Tori chuckled.

"See, that would be a problem." Jewell shrugged. "Maybe someday."

Jillian took a drink of her coffee, "Drake and I haven't really talked about it. I'm in Jewell's camp. Maybe someday."

All eyes turned to Jade. "What? Kids? Me? Ah, that would be a big *no*. They scare the shit out of me."

"They scare the shit out of all of us." Ember laughed and reached for a small crescent roll. "They don't come with a manual or a programming script. We all play it by ear and hope for the best."

"Well, see, that right there, that sucks. Manuals should be mandatory." Jade got up and headed back to get seconds. She lifted the dome cover off a dish. "Jazz, I think I love you. Look at the size of these strawberries! In December!"

CHAPTER 3

Ember sat in the pew and watched as Dr. Maliki Blue and Poet Campbell exchanged vows. Poet's dress was simple and breathtaking at the same time. A silk sheath with an ivory lace overlay that fit her athletic body like a glove. For the third or fourth thousand time since puberty, Ember wished she had that type of figure. Poet, Keelee, Tori, all the King women... tall, slender, and minus the curves that were the bane of her existence. But Joseph really loved her curves. She slid her attention from the couple to her husband. The Tom Ford tux was stunning, not in small part due to the man underneath the fabric. Her husband. As if he sensed her looking, Joey's eyes

PROMISES

found hers. The smoldering intensity of his gaze still took her breath away.

As soon as Mal and Poet turned and made their way down the aisle, Jasmine and Chad exited the sanctuary in the opposite direction. Chad's song had been beautiful and she wished they could stay for the reception, but Chad wanted the event to remain focused on Mal and Poet, and with his celebrity, it probably wouldn't have if they'd stayed.

Ember leaned over to Faith, who had been sitting beside her during the ceremony. "I'm concerned about the photographer." She'd been watching the man snap pictures during the ceremony. Pictures that included Joey.

Faith glanced over at the man and smiled. "That's Paul. He works for Guardian. It was one of the things Jason required of Mal for the wedding. He's taken family pictures of us and of Reece's birthday parties. Those pictures are going to be scrubbed. Just like the guest list was."

Ember blinked. "Guardian vetted the wedding guests?"

"Every last one of them," Faith chuckled. "You get used to it."

"I guess." Ember's gaze swept over the people in

the church. She saw it then. The security teams around the outside of the crowd. Men in suits that were not engaged in conversation but were actively watching the crowd. Wow, she'd been at the ranch and then at The Rose for so long she had forgotten the steps taken to protect the Kings that worked in D.C.

Faith nodded to Joseph, who'd escorted the maid of honor to the narthex of the church. "Is Joseph going to the reception with the wedding party?"

"Yes, all four of them are riding in the limo. I was going to catch a ride with someone."

"You can ride with us." Faith tapped Jason on the shoulder. He turned from his conversation with Jacob and put his arm around his wife. "Ember is going to ride with us to the reception, okay?"

"Absolutely." Jason smiled at Ember. "He wore a tux."

Jacob smiled and nodded at the photographer. "I have proof."

"I want a copy of every picture of him wearing it, please!" Ember smiled widely at the thought of framing a picture of them together in formal wear.

The photographer had taken several of them together before the ceremony.

∼

Mal and Poet entered the reception to rousing applause. Maliki swept her into his arms and they danced their first dance together as man and wife.

Ember felt Joseph behind her. She leaned back into his arms.

"Have I told you today how much I love you?" he whispered against her hair.

"I *think* you said you loved me when I left the room this morning for breakfast." Joey's fingers rippled over her ribs, tickling her. She wiggled away from him, laughing. "Go, you have to do the best man thing. You are required to give a toast, you know."

Joey rolled his eyes and then closed them. "Oh, that hurt, didn't it? Poor baby." Ember cupped his cheek with her hand. "Not quite recovered?"

He opened one eye. "Recovered enough to want to eat you alive."

"There's my big, bad wolf. Go do what you need to do. We can feast later."

"It was a lovely wedding, wasn't it?" Ember's head laid against Joey's shoulder as they moved across the dance floor later that night. The tux he wore fit perfectly. She ran her hand down the fine wool fabric. He could have posed for a fashion spread. His dark good looks and the silver at his temples plus the Adonis body. Joey was her first and only true love. The man was fierce and hovered, but there wasn't a better father or husband on the planet.

"Mmm..." That was Joseph talk for it was okay and not as big of a deal as he made it out to be, but he'd never admit it.

"How do you feel?" Ember leaned away a bit and gazed up at him.

"Perfect when you are in my arms." He leaned down and kissed her. The possession in his kiss hadn't changed in the years since they'd married. He made her feel cherished and needed every moment of every day.

Ember smiled up at him when he lifted away. "Did you ever think we'd have a chance at being this happy?"

Joseph shook his head and moved them out of

another couple's way with fluid grace. "Never, that's why I cherish every minute with you. I can't wait to have you to myself for the next two weeks."

"You say the most remarkable things." She sighed against him. Obviously, he didn't remember inviting everyone they knew to Aruba. As much as she didn't want to shatter his illusion for the future, she needed to remind him of what he'd done. Ember stopped moving and stared up at him, her eyes narrowed and searching, just to be positively sure he wasn't playing with her.

"What? Is something wrong? Do you need a doctor?" He cupped her cheek in his hand and scrutinized her.

"No, I'm not the one who is going to need a doctor. Do you remember what happened last night?"

"Too much bourbon. Thank God everyone I give a fuck about has now done the wedding thing. I'm not doing that again." He stared down at her. "What?"

"Joey, you invited everyone to Aruba. With us. As in, everyone is planning to fly down after the wedding."

He stopped. "No, I didn't."

"You did. Gabriel and Jason worked all day

today to cover responsibilities. From what the Coven told me, everyone is coming. Even Joy and Dixon."

"I didn't *invite* anyone." He ground the words out through his clenched teeth. There was no way on God's green earth that he would have... His eyes cut to Dixon and Drake, who were talking with Mike. He searched for Jacob and found him on the dance floor with Tori. "The motherfucking bastards."

He grabbed Ember's hand and weaved through the dancing couples. He stood directly behind Jacob and dropped a hand on his brother's shoulder. The little shit's smile dropped as soon as he looked around. "Hey, what's up?"

"What's up is that I'm going to kill you." Joseph shoved a finger in his brother's chest. "You and that dynamic duo of horse shit put this all together. It was your brainchild to have a drinking game. You set me up."

Jacob's eyes flared before he smiled. "It only took you twenty hours to figure that out? Damn, old man, you're slipping."

"The only thing that will slip is my hands around your throat." The low threat made his brother's face pale a bit.

"It was Double D's idea." Jacob pointed to his men. "If you kill me, kill them, too."

"Nobody is getting killed." Ember grabbed her husband's arm. "It serves you right for drinking like a teenager."

"Yeah, what she said." Jacob smiled and nodded.

"Jacob, please, don't make this worse." Tori stood in front of her husband. "You are just as much to blame as he is, Joseph. Imagine what a world this would be if you both grew up."

"What she said," Ember agreed with Tori.

Joseph jerked his head toward her. "You're okay with this?"

Ember nodded. "I don't have a problem with it at all. We'll have our evenings together. All alone. All night. Every night. We have more than enough parents to take turns watching our son. Our nights *alone*. Nonnegotiable."

Tori agreed. "Right, we already talked about that."

"We?" Joseph shot a glance between the two women.

"The Coven," Ember filled him in. "Like I said, they are all coming."

"We don't have enough rooms." Joseph crossed

his arms and gave his brother another pointed glare.

"Gabriel rented a villa about a mile away. Frank and Amanda are planning on staying there, and whoever arrives after the house fills up will be welcome, too." Tori shrugged. "It's settled. Getting into a pissing contest at Mal and Poet's wedding will not change anything."

Ember's husband's jaw clenched as he stared at his brother. "Just know that payback is a bitch, little man."

Jacob smiled. "I can't wait." His laughter floated around them.

Ember glanced at Tori, who sighed and shook her head. "For God's sake, Jacob, stop poking the tiger." Tori pulled Jacob away as Jason and Faith danced by. The smile on Jason's face narrowed Joey's eyes even further. "My entire family was in on it. So be it. They'll pay for it. Individually or together, I'll make them pay for this little prank."

"What are you plotting?"

"Revenge." He smiled down at her. "Sweet, unadulterated revenge."

She lifted her eyebrows. "Nobody gets hurt."

Joseph shrugged. "Not my fault they started it. I'll finish it."

"Let me clarify, Joey. Family equals no blood, no loss of limbs, no weapons, no one gets physically hurt or emotionally scarred."

"Noted." He stepped back and led her in a waltz. A sneer spread across his face.

Oh, dear, that didn't bode well for anyone. What had those idiots done?

CHAPTER 4

Joseph strode down the long hallway to the kitchen. "Consuela." He enfolded the small, birdlike woman into his arms. She never changed. She was always flitting about with a smile on her face. The woman was a beam of sunshine that had been with him since he bought the residence years ago.

"Oh sir, it is good to see you." She peeked behind him. "The missus is not here?"

Joseph motioned to the table. "She's upstairs unpacking and taking a shower. She told me she called about the unexpected guests we'd be having?"

"Oh, yes. I have many hands to help. I stocked the pantry, the linens are fresh, and the rooms have been aired out. I prepare us for your family, sir. I'm happy that the house is filled with laughter again." Her angelic face beamed up at him.

"Right." He rubbed his neck. "I wanted to have a private celebration with the missus. We are expecting our second child."

Consuela closed her eyes and clasped her hands to her chest. "Praise be, sir. Blessings on all of you."

"Ah, thank you. I'm going to need your help. They blew my plans to he... ah... smithereens when my brothers decided they were going to encroach on my vacation."

"Of course, sir. Anything you need." Consuela smiled up at him.

"All right, now, this is going to be a secret, so you can't tell a soul."

"Even José, sir?" She mentioned her husband, who also worked for him.

"No, you'll need to tell José everything and we'll need to meet several times to make sure this comes together."

"Of course! Anything, sir. Anything." Consuela flew across the kitchen for a pad of paper and pencil. "What do you need?"

A self-satisfied smile spread across his face. Yeah, he was going to have every one of those assholes pulling rabbits out of their asses. *Fuck with my private time with my woman and you will pay.*

~

The vast window to the ocean was open and the white gauze curtains fluttered in the constant onshore breeze. Joseph shut the doors firmly behind him and locked them. He had no idea when the horde would descend, but before they did, he was spending some quality time with Ember. Exhausted after the reception, Ember had fallen asleep before he'd taken off his tux. He glanced at the closet. He had to admit the suit fit him well, and the way Ember had looked at him when he'd stood up on that dais—he didn't mind the cost. It was worth every penny.

He unbuttoned his white cotton shirt and dropped it on a chair on the way to the bathroom. The soft fall of water told him where his wife was. He dropped his slacks and kicked them toward the wall. He turned the corner and focused on the steamed-up glass of the shower. Ember's soft curves beyond the glass called to him as strongly as they had when he was a randy teenager. He kicked off his boxers and pulled the door open, stepping into a cloud of steam.

Ember turned around and smiled. That happiness in her eyes, it was his drug of choice. He'd do anything in the world to keep it there. "Hi, Momma." He reached for her and pulled her into him. Soon, her stomach would swell with their baby. For a man who'd spent most of his adult life dispensing death, the miracle of birth fascinated him.

"Hi, Daddy." She wound her arms around his neck. "I'm going to get fat again."

"You were never fat." He leaned down and kissed her. "I loved seeing Blake grow inside you."

He tucked her close and tightened his grip on her. He'd tabled their normal lovemaking the second he found out she was pregnant. There was no way he'd stress *her* body or *their* baby because of his kink. The love he had for his wife was enough. Hell, it was more than enough, and if Ember never wanted to get her freak on again, he'd live a fulfilled, happy life. Admitting that to himself had been... liberating. Being normal—well... normal-ish, having what some would call a day job and working to grow Guardian's elite was fulfilling, but it was Ember and Blake that had tamed the inner beast that had always dwelled deep inside him.

"Are you upset?" Ember arched her back and looked up at him.

He blinked at her question. "At what?"

"Oh, gee, do you want me to list the reasons? Our unplanned pregnancy? Your brothers and family inviting themselves down? I know they tricked you into inviting them." Ember chuckled. "Maybe at not having me naked all day long or having the house and beach to ourselves. Take your pick."

He rolled his eyes and grabbed her shampoo, dispensing a palmful into his hand. "I told you exactly how happy I was that we are having another baby. Planned or not." He turned her around and worked the shampoo through her hair. She moaned and reached back, holding his hips as she tipped her head back. Her soft ass pushed into his hardening cock. He leaned forward and whispered in her ear. "I love the idea of another child. I want Blake to have a little brother or sister, and I'd love to have as many kids as you're willing to give me. I love you." He kissed her temple and walked them forward into the water's spray to work the suds out of her hair.

She wiped the water out of her eyes and blinked up at him. "What about your family showing up?"

He turned her around and grabbed the soap. He lathered it in his hands as he stared at her. "I don't want to talk about my family right now."

Ember smiled. "No? What do you want to talk about?"

"Absolutely nothing." He reached forward and caressed her skin with his soapy hands. She waggled her eyebrows and grabbed his shaft. He jerked when she rolled his balls in her hand. He fused their lips together and backed her into the cold tile of the shower wall. Her soft gasp as the cold registered flicked his desire higher. He braced his feet and reached down, cupping her ass. He lifted her, sliding her up the wet tile until she could wrap her legs around him.

He stared at the rose flush the hot water and desire had placed on her chest, neck, and face. She reached between them and centered his cock under her core. He shook his head. "You're not ready yet."

She loosened her legs and her body dropped onto the head of his shaft. Her heat gripped him. His eyes closed in pleasure. Her lips next to his ear whispered, "Oh, believe me, I'm ready. I don't know what you're going to do with your wife, Mr. King. She has been unnaturally horny during this first trimester. Her hormones are running amok."

"I guess I must endure her urges. Take one for the team, so to speak." He flexed his hips and slid deeper inside of his wife.

"You must take more than one, slugger. Momma wants sex all the time." She leaned in and sucked his bottom lip between her teeth and bit down, sending a lightning bolt of lust through him. Still, he held her carefully. As much as she assured him that sex couldn't hurt the baby, the inner caveman-slash-protector in him refused to take her too deep or too hard. Ember was his life. His family was the reason he'd lived; hell, he'd done more than lived, he'd flourished. He'd die before he'd let anyone hurt them.

Their bodies worked together in a coordinated dance. He broke free from their kiss and inhaled tremendous pulls of air. Her nails dug into the skin of his back. The sting catapulted him toward that fucking cliff. He felt her body contract as she neared her own climax. He slipped a hand from under her and found the swell of her breast. His fingers tightened on the nipple and he squeezed slightly.

"Joey." Ember gasped his name seconds before her body seized around him. She clung to him as he moved in and out of her warm body, chasing his own release. He lowered his head to her shoulder and kissed, then bit the juncture of her neck and shoulder as he came.

"So good." Her words between gasps for oxygen satisfied that inner caveman, even if he didn't let the bastard out to play. He shifted, made sure she was okay, and slowly lowered her to her feet, giving her support to stand until she found her legs again.

He pulled her into him and rocked with her under the warm water. "I love you." She murmured her words against his chest, but he understood them. Hell, he knew the truth of those words down into the smallest atom of his DNA.

He smoothed her hair away from her neck and slid his hand around the fragile column. Tipping her head back, he waited for those beautiful eyes to open. "I love you more than my life itself. I want as many babies as you'll give me. My family is a pain in the ass, but they always have been. I'm not mad. I'm not upset. I'm in love with you and I'm going to be a dad again. I never thought I could be this happy, and that's all due to you. Because you cared enough to take a chance on me and come to Aruba all those years ago."

"I'd do it again. Over and over."

He smiled. "Good." He slowly lowered to one knee. "Ember King, would you do me the honor of renewing your vows with me next week on the beach in front of our pain in the ass family which will probably include about a dozen screaming children, give or take?"

She tipped her head back and laughed before she leaned forward. "Joseph King, I would love to renew my vows with you." She cupped his cheeks and kissed him. "Your family would never believe what a hopeless romantic you are."

He stood and turned off the water, grabbing a bath sheet to wrap her in. A smile spread across his face. "Oh, I think they'll figure it out."

Ember let him tuck in the bath sheet's corner after he twirled her up in it. "What are you doing?" She arched an eyebrow. "You're up to something."

He grabbed a smaller towel and wrapped it around his hips. "I am."

She pointed a finger at him. "No bodily injuries."

"None."

"Are you going to give me a hint?"

He shook his head and grabbed her hand, pulling her into the huge master suite and the soft bed that faced the ocean. "Not even a little one." God only knew when his dipshit brothers and crazy sisters would arrive. Until that time, he was going to spend every minute he could naked next to the woman he loved.

CHAPTER 5

"What am I looking at?" Jason leaned back in his chair and peered over his tablet at his sister.

"That's a good question. I don't know." Jewell pulled a pencil out of her hair and bit down on the eraser.

"Okay, let me rephrase that. Why are you showing me this portion of... code?" He'd taken a wild ass guess that the nonsense on the screen in front of him was some variation of computer language.

"Oh, well, when Tempest mentioned to Jacob that one of the Fates was still trying to get into a clone of the hard drive that we recovered from Vista, I went back and took another look at the information that would be available to them and what we've done to mitigate the data contained on the drive."

"That sounds smart. I take it you found something?"

Jewell shook her head and said yes at the same time. Jason took off his glasses and pinched the bridge of his nose. God, he could hardly wait to board the plane to Aruba tomorrow. He needed to plant his ass on the sandy beach and let the waves take every concern away. But for now, he had to play twenty guesses with his sister, who didn't have a clue she was pissing him off. "Explain that, please."

"Well, everything on the drive we've scrubbed, and except for the information that I've already reported to you, we've patched all the holes."

"Okay…" He stared at his sister. Her gaze focused somewhere over his shoulder. "Where's Zane?" It was so much easier to get to the point when her husband was present. He was the 'Jewell Whisperer' and worth his fucking weight in titanium.

"What? Zane? Oh, he's out buying a few things for Aruba. You're going, right?" She looked at him and blinked owlishly.

"Yes, we are going. You were saying?"

"Huh?"

"About the hard drive?" He nodded to her tablet.

"Oh, yeah, I wanted to make sure we had everything covered, so I used the new program that we've developed and we measured the order of magnitude in the code which, for the information that was on the drive and the functionality contained in the programs, should have been substantially less than it was. So, it was either a lack of cohesion and out of sync with its functionality, or someone put the extraneous code where it is for a reason."

"You believe he put it there on purpose." Somehow the gift of that damn Russian hacker kept on giving, didn't it?

Jewell nodded. "Yeah, I do. Using function point as the standard, some of the code is extraneous. But in all the time I dealt with Vista, I never knew him to do anything without a reason."

Jason leaned forward. "What did you find in the code?"

Jewell sighed. "Nothing yet. I'm going to work on this while we are in Aruba, I mean, if you will allow me to put it onto my laptop. I'm the only person who can access the information and I never hook it up to unsecured servers."

"Permission granted. I know you'll safeguard the information. Do you have your team ready for your unannounced vacation?"

"I do. Well, Zane does. He handles the scheduling and stuff. Did you know it was eighty-three degrees today in Aruba? Eighty-three, Jase. I so need to thaw the heck out, I really do." Jewell shoved her hand into the front pocket of her fluffy hoodie. "Winter has been hard this year."

"The year has been a bitch on too many levels, winter weather included. We all deserve a break." He leaned back in his chair.

"The cleanup of the Fates' shit is going to take years. Stratus is probably crawling under rocks and trying to figure out who the hell is going to lead them now." Jewell stood and stomped her foot, sending her jeans down over her high-heeled boots. "I guess that's job security for us, huh?"

"I'd be happy if we worked ourselves out of a job." Jason stood and ambled to the door with his sister. "See you at the airport?"

"Yep. I get to hold Royce all the way. Faith already said I could." Jewell did a little jig. "That little boy is a cuddle bug."

"He is." Jason smiled at his sister and opened the door.

"See you in the morning." Jewell waved at Sonya and let herself out the double doors.

Sonya turned and Jason tipped his head, silently asking her to come into his office. The woman stood on the stilts she called heels and wobbled into the office.

"Do you have everything you need?" Jason nodded to the computer. "I've reviewed all the documents you flagged. Is my laptop synced?"

"IT is on their way up with it. I wanted to make sure they'd installed and function-checked the latest crypto programs. Jewell is going with you, right?" Sonya looked up from her notepad.

"Yes, the entire family is converging."

"Good, then you'll have a secure hookup. I'll forward the important things and rack and stack the busy work unless you tell me to let it dribble toward you."

"Rack and stack is fine. If I go out of my mind with boredom, I'm sure Faith will have plenty of things planned to keep me busy. She was on the official Aruba website this morning looking at tours, places to see, and things to do. With all the aunts, uncles, and cousins, I'm hoping I'll be able to spend some quality time alone with her." Jason picked up his briefcase.

"I hope so. I really do. I don't know a person who works harder than you do." Sonya handed him a small yellow square of paper. "The address you wanted."

He glanced at her, confused until he saw her flowery handwriting. She'd found him a daily meeting on Aruba. "You're the best." He hugged the tiny woman carefully.

"You're damn right I am. Now, get out of here. I'm going to take some time off while you're gone. I have Christmas shopping to do and then I have to wrap it all. Send me some sunshine, would you?" They walked to the door together.

"I'll figure out a way to make that happen," Jason chuckled, not at the absurdity of sending sunshine to someone but because he'd already purchased Sonya and her husband Mark a trip to St. John for a Christmas present and worked behind her back with HR to get someone to fill in for the two weeks she'd be gone in January. Her husband knew, but she didn't.

"You see that you do. Now, go. I'm going to close up shop and go home. I want to curl up in front of the fireplace with my husband." Sonya waved him away and sat down. She glanced up at him. "Why are you still here? The sooner you leave, the sooner I can leave."

"Computer?" He chuckled at her pole-axed expression.

The door opened and Hilde, the runner from IT, hustled in. "I'm not late, am I?" She glanced at her watch and then to the clock on the wall.

"No, I'm in a rush to start my vacation." Jason extended his hand and Hilde handed over his computer. He slid it into his briefcase and smiled at both ladies. "I'll see you in two weeks." Knowing he wasn't coming back in those double doors for two glorious weeks settled a sense of freedom around him. He hadn't taken two full weeks off in… well, not in a long, long time.

∼

Faith held Royce as he slept. She should put him down, but… His long, dark lashes rested on his chubby cheeks. The little boy was a duplicate of his daddy, down to the curly hair and arched eyebrows. Royce was just over a year old. She closed her eyes and rocked with her precious baby in her arms. Her life was nothing like she'd imagined it would be. Jason had given her the world. More than anyone could ask for, and he loved Reece as much as he loved Royce.

She gazed down at the little one in her arms. Being a mother and wife filled her life with happiness. She had her friends she'd made on the PTA and all the moms on the teams that Reece played on.

Her eyes traveled around the nursery. A big difference from her small trailer in Savannah, Georgia. She didn't miss that old trailer, even though she was proud of what she'd accomplished and how she'd been able to take care of Reece. No, she missed nothing of her past life, except Helena and Cal. They were still in Savannah. Faith called Helena—or she called Faith—at least once a week. They had promoted Cal to Sergeant, so his hours were better. He'd decided against joining Guardian because he preferred to work at the community level. God, all the worry, the scrimping and saving, getting Reece to school or to daycare, and stressing about how to pay for college was in the past. She lifted her eyes and said a prayer of thanks again. Her life was blessed beyond measure and beyond her wildest dreams.

She heard the front door alarm chirp and the

door open. Jason's low voice as Tippy and Tommy greeted him at the door put a smile on her face. Tommy was the golden retriever that Grandpa Marshall had given the boys last Christmas. He was a wonderful dog with a calm demeanor but was very protective of both boys.

"Is he asleep?" Jason asked in a hushed voice as he entered the nursery.

"Just now." She handed the toddler to her husband and watched as he lifted Royce and kissed his forehead. He drifted across the room, cuddling his boy as he moved. He carefully laid the little boy down and pulled his blanket over him, kissing his head one more time before he straightened.

He made his way back across the room, and after ushering the dogs out of the way, he helped her up out of the rocker and pulled her into his arms. "Hello, Mrs. King. How are you feeling?" He leaned down and kissed her, pulling her into that massive, tight body. She relaxed in his arms and enjoyed the rare moment of peace.

When he lifted away, she smiled up at him. "Hello, Mr. King. I'm fine. I see you got off work at a decent hour." She tipped her head toward the door. "Shall we move this conversation so the little man doesn't wake up?"

He smiled and glanced over at his sleeping son again. "Speaking of my little men, where is Reece?" He released her from his hold but linked their hands as they left the nursery.

"He's with Frank and Amanda. The boys are having a sleepover at Jacob and Tori's. Jacob will pick them up from Amanda after he takes all the dogs to doggy daycare. He and Jared are taking the animals to the facility. They should be here to pick up Tippy and Tommy at six."

"I'm glad they found someone to take care of all of them."

"Right? The boys wanted to bring them, but Jacob promised he'd find a nice place. They have video cameras that we can tap into that show the boys their puppies are having fun."

"I never would have believed it. We are one of those couples, Faith. We take our dogs to doggy daycare." He rolled his eyes.

"We do, but only when we are out of town. The boys are happy and distracted. Amanda was going to find out what they wanted to do on Aruba after their school day is over."

"Hopefully, they won't plan a coup and take over the island." Jason led them into the bedroom and stripped off his tie with his free hand.

"That was not on the list of options she was going to give them, although it may come in a close second to snorkeling. Grandpa Frank has purchased snorkel gear for everyone."

Jason chuckled. "Of course, he has. That man pretends he's a cantankerous old fart, but he's a marshmallow when it comes to his grandchildren."

"He is." She sat down on the bed and watched as he stripped out of the suit he wore. He reached for a t-shirt and she cleared her throat. "Reece is out of the house. Royce is asleep."

Jason looked over his shoulder and blinked at her. "I didn't want to assume. You've been so tired lately. What did the doctor say? Your appointment was this morning, right?"

He turned, his erection thick and hard. She smiled at him and patted the bed beside her. "Yes. It turns out there is a reason I've been so tired." She closed her eyes and shook her head. Such a logical reason.

He was beside her in a second, on his knees by the bed. "What? Are you okay? Please tell me you're okay, babe." He reached a shaking hand for hers.

"I'm fine." She smiled at him. "We need to make a list of R names again."

One second she was sitting up in the bed, the next she was on her back with six feet, seven inches of chiseled, god-like muscles hovering over her. "We're pregnant?"

"We are."

He cupped her face and kissed her a hundred times, all the while laughing with her. She slid her legs open and cradled him between them.

"Wait? How did this happen?"

Faith laughed at his astonished face and joked, "Well, the usual way, I think."

"You know what I mean."

She shrugged under him. "Evidently, you have fertile swimmers. Remember when we went to Savannah for Halloween so Reece could trick-or-treat around the old neighborhood? I forgot my pills. I told you that, right?" His eyes narrowed, and he nodded. "Well, I doubled up on them when we got home. I've done it before, and we've never gotten pregnant. We hit the jackpot this time. The doctor gave me some prenatal vitamins, I was a bit anemic. That's why I'm so tired."

"We'll get you help with Reece and Royce."

"I don't need or want help."

"At least until you feel better."

"I feel fine. I'm going to Aruba for two weeks

and I'm going to relax, lay in the shade, and watch my boys play."

Jason smiled down at her. "So, you're okay."

"Very." She lifted her hips under him. "But I can think of ways I could be better."

"Anything for you."

She let him undress her and make love to her. His touch was reverent and gentle. He whispered his love to her between kisses and made sure her body was ready for him. Her husband, the man she couldn't imagine living without, treated her like she was priceless and irreplaceable. She closed her eyes as he entered her and let the tears of joy fall. He kissed the trail away. His love erased the past and paved their future. He was their world, and he gladly accepted that mantle.

She climaxed and shattered around him as he found his own release. He held his massive body over her as they came down from the high from which he'd taken them. He rolled and brought her with him. "We're pregnant."

"We are."

"Do we know if it is a boy or a girl yet?"

She laughed. "No, I have an appointment when we get back, before the boys and I go to South Dakota for Christmas break."

He popped up on his elbows. "I don't want you flying without me."

She chuckled and snuggled closer to him. "Then fly us there, Superman."

She felt him stroke her hair and kiss her forehead and heard him whisper, "Anything for you, princess. Anything."

CHAPTER 6

Justin King opened the door to his New York apartment and stopped halfway inside. His wolf-whistle pierced the air. His wife smiled and bounced over to him. "Do you like it?" She spun, showing him her ensemble.

"I do, is it new?" She'd stopped the zipper of the skintight pink wetsuit halfway up and her breasts threatened to spill out. All in all, it was an extremely enticing sight.

"Yes, I have one for you, too. Not pink, though." She rushed to the couch and pulled a wetsuit from a box. His was royal blue. "It is the latest tech. Precisely distributed stretch compression around all the primary muscle groups. From the research I did, they are mimicking the tech used for Olympic swimmers."

Justin took the suit she offered him. "And you got this for me because…?" The material was ultra-light.

"Well, it was going to be a Christmas gift, but since we are going to Aruba, I figured you could use it."

He chuckled. "For what, snorkeling? I don't think we need a wetsuit for that."

"That's what I thought until I found some cool things to do around Aruba."

Justin put his suit on the back of the couch and wrapped his arms around his wife's waist. The material under his fingers hugged her tight body like a second skin. "Cool things to do? I can think of several things to do that don't require any clothes."

"Really?" She wrapped her arms around his neck. "I think the people who operate the water jet packs would object." Dani lifted on her toes and kissed him.

He frowned at her. "Water jet pack?"

Her smile was radiant. She knew she had his interest. "Think James Bond jet pack but powered by water. They have a company in the Dominican Republic that offers lessons and rentals."

"But we're going to Aruba."

"The DR is an hour and a half by plane. A day trip. We can schedule it for one day that we don't have aunt and uncle duties."

He jerked his head up. "Wait, what?"

"Well, the Coven has agreed that we'd take turns with the kids so each of the couples gets some alone time."

He opened his mouth and then shut it again before he stepped away from her and put his hands on his hips. "We don't have children, why should we watch everyone else's?"

Dani popped him on the arm and rounded the couch to grab her laptop. "Because it is the right thing to do and we're family, silly." She clicked the touchpad and activated the screen. "See, here is the information for the Dominican Republic, here is information on kite surfing. I really want to try that. They offer it in Aruba and there are forty-two registered dive sites around the island. We can rent tanks or ship ours to Joseph's. It would be expensive, but I'd rather ship ours." She glanced up at him and stopped. "What?"

"All day?"

She looked at him and narrowed her eyes. "I'm sorry, I don't follow."

"We're going to have the kids all day long?"

"Yes, Justin. All day. We'll have the older kids along with another couple, so there will be plenty of eyes to watch them. We agreed the babies would stay at the house and Ember said their housekeeper has nieces that would help in the evenings so we adults can lounge around the pool and have cocktails. Besides, we can go snorkeling with the older kids. It will be fun."

Justin rubbed the back of his neck. He loved his brothers' and sister's kids, but he had zero experience being a supervisory element for anything under the age of 18, as in adults. "Uh, okay."

Dani put the computer down and rounded the couch toward him. "What's wrong?"

"What if I break one or something?" He dropped his head back and sighed audibly. "Kids break, don't they?"

"No, children don't break. I'll be there along with one of your brothers or sisters." Dani wrapped her arms around his waist.

"Great, it would be my luck we'll pull the short stick and end up with Jade and Nic." He could just picture it now. Jade teaching the kids how to throw punches and how to sneak up on someone and throw them to the ground.

"Nic loves kids, and he's great with them. You handle an international corporation, base jump off mountains, swim with sharks, and do things we don't talk about. A handful of kids are nothing." She smiled up at him.

"Handful? Have you seen the tribe the Kings and Marshalls have started?" He did a mental count. "If you don't count the babies, there are eight ankle biters. Eight. Even if we have another couple with us that is two kids per person to watch in the water. What if they drown?"

"Justin, I promise we won't break anyone or let anyone drown."

Her shoulders moved up and down under his hands. He glared down at her. "I can't believe you're laughing at me."

"I can't believe you're being a baby about this."

"Oh, no, not fair, I'm not being a baby." He wasn't. He was being cautious. Which, all things considered, wasn't a word that he applied to himself. Ever.

She stepped away from him and walked backward toward the hall that led to the bedroom. "Right, you're not being a baby. You're being a…

coward." She lifted her eyebrows at him and slid the zipper of her wetsuit down as far as it would go. Fuck, she was gloriously naked underneath all that pink neoprene.

"Coward?" He stalked forward while pulling his suit jacket off.

"Mmm..." She slipped out of the arms of the suit and again walked backward.

He pulled his silk tie off and unfastened his cufflinks as he pursued her down the long hallway. By the time they'd played cat and mouse into their bedroom, he'd unfastened the buttons of his linen shirt and pulled the tails from his slacks. Dani turned around and slid the wetsuit from her body, revealing all her glorious skin. He was behind her in a moment, wrapping her in his arms.

"I am many things, but never a coward." He leaned in and gently bit the juncture of her neck and shoulder.

"Ah... admit it, you're afraid of those kids."

"Never."

"Really?" She spun in his arms and found his belt buckle. She undid the fastener as she stared up at him.

"Really."

"Then maybe we should consider having one of our own."

He settled his hands on her waist. "I thought…" She reached in his slacks and under the waistband of his boxers.

"Use your words, King." She cupped his shaft and stroked it from base to tip.

He wrapped his arms around her and captured her lips. He craved his woman, needed her in ways he still couldn't comprehend. When she ended the kiss, she sighed, "Okay, no words."

Keeping her in his arms, he moved her backward toward the bed. He leaned over, half pushing, half placing her on the bed. Her legs came up, and he grabbed them, pulling her ass to the edge of the bed. He entered her and bent over her, pinning her to the mattress. "You shouldn't tease me." He withdrew and slammed into her. "I face my fears. Kids included."

"I know." She panted the words and pulled him down for a kiss. He let her lead the kiss while his hips pumped hard and fast. She was tight and wet, the heat and clinging slide into and out of her body taking him precariously close to orgasm too damn fast. He lifted slightly from the kiss to breathe.

"God, so good. So good." Dani's breathless

words against his lips. He repositioned his arms so they were tucked under her, grabbed her shoulders, and used the brace against her body for more leverage. He stared at her, still mesmerized by the way her body reacted to him, the blush that spread from her chest up her neck and to her face as she neared her climax. He'd watched her countless times, and each time they made love, he found something new to admire. She arched under him and grabbed his shoulders. He adjusted and thrust harder, knowing they both were close. Her body tightened around him. He stared as her eyes closed and her body contracted around him. He pulled her tight against him and bucked into her, stilling only after he found his release.

Her hands trailed over his upper back. He lifted away from her, stopping to kiss her soft lips. They both crawled to the middle of the king-sized bed and collapsed, wrapped in each other's arms. He pulled his hand through her waves of hair and sighed, "I'm not afraid of children."

Her laughter bubbled around them. "I know. How else was I going to get you to stalk me down the hallway and take me like a caveman?"

He lifted away from her. "Seriously? How about saying, 'Hey, I want caveman sex'?"

Dani laughed again. "Duly noted. Caveman sex. Maybe we can have a code word for that. It would be awkward in a crowd."

He chuckled and dropped back down to the bed and pulled her on top of his chest. "Yeah, like Neanderthal or sabretooth tiger."

Dani shook her head. "Too hard to work into a conversation. Oh! I could just call you Tiger."

"Tiger, huh?"

"Yeah." She smiled wide and lifted her eyebrows a couple times. "But I was serious. Maybe we could think about starting our own family."

He stared at her for a moment, letting the sincerity of her words cover him. He blinked back the surprise. "Starting a family would mean no more adventures." They'd spent most of their lives together finding the next extreme event to take part in. They were self-admitted adrenaline junkies and unapologetic in those pursuits.

"I've been thinking about that. We are extremely conscientious. We have the best safety gear money can buy. The likelihood of us getting hit by lightning, or heck, a bus or a car is higher than us getting hurt doing the things we train for months to do."

He pushed her hair back from her face. "I want a family with you."

"But…" She cocked her head and waited.

"But I'm not sure." There. He'd said it. "What if something happens to me?"

Dani played with the hair on his chest. "You mean like what happened to your father?"

He nodded. "My dad left my mom with eight kids."

"Well, first off, we are not having eight kids." Dani smiled down at him. "How about we start with one?"

He gave a half-hearted smile. "Point taken."

She shimmied up his body and dropped her elbows by his head, making direct eye contact with him. "No one knows the future. We could live to be a hundred or we could die tomorrow. I'm positive you'd make a wonderful father. I've seen you with your nieces and nephews."

He held her eyes but shook his head slightly. "You can't know that."

She smiled down at him. "Just like you can't know you won't be. Look, I'm not trying to rush you into anything. Take all the time you need. If you think about it and you're still not sure or you don't want to have kids yet, that's fine. Starting a family isn't something one of us decides. We both need to be ready."

"How did I ever get so lucky?" He wrapped his hand behind her neck and brought her down for a kiss.

She pulled away and whispered against his lips, "We weren't lucky, Mr. King. What we have—it was destiny."

CHAPTER 7

Zane opened the last cabinet in the bathroom. *Not there.* Damn it, he'd bought extra toothpaste. He remembered it distinctly. "Babe, where did you put the toothpaste?"

Not getting an answer, he popped his head out of the bathroom. "Jewell?"

"Huh?" The distracted call came from the living room.

He sighed and padded down the hallway. "Babe, where did you put the extra tube of toothpaste?"

She blinked up from her cross-legged position. "The what?"

"Toothpaste," Zane repeated.

"Ah… try the maintenance cabinet." She stared

down at the tablet, once again lost in the program she was working.

"Maintenance cabinet. Perfectly logical." *For his wife and about three other people in the world with her intelligence.* He muttered the words as he spun on his heel and headed toward the small cabinet that held the hammer, screwdrivers, tape measures, and the odds and ends that they used to fix up things around the apartment. And there it was. He grabbed the boxed tube of minty freshness and shut the cabinet. He started to go into the bedroom to finish packing for them but stopped short. *No. He had to ask.*

"Babe." He waited to see if she heard him.

She blinked up at him. "Wasn't it there?"

"It was, but I have to ask… why did you put it there?"

"Oh, we had a full tube in the bathroom, and I read somewhere you could use toothpaste to patch holes in the wall." She lowered her head and ran a finger across her tablet. "Why would he put the same code in twice?"

Zane sat down beside her. "Who are we talking about?"

Jewell dropped her tablet to the couch. "Vista."

"Okay, let's assume I don't know what you're

talking about. Start at the beginning." He had no earthly clue what she was talking about, but the name Vista rang every warning bell he owned.

Jewell sighed heavily. "When Tempest was debriefing the Fate in Russia, she said that One had the hard drive. We are surmising the drive I had was the original, but if there was a clone or a ghost of that hard drive kept for security…"

"You do that. You ghost all of your hard drives." He'd seen her do it.

"Right, so if they fail, I have the programs already loaded on another drive and partitioned exactly how I want it to be. But ghosting the drives is insurance against failure, so you can recreate your systems with little problem. If that is what they have, we have no worries. But if he cloned the hard drive, the Fate or whoever has access to it would have access to the information we found on Vista's drive."

"But we—and by we, I mean you—have mitigated all the damage knowledge of that information could cause." Zane reached over and rubbed her back. She leaned into his touch and then literally fell into his side.

"But what if I haven't?" She sighed again and looked up at him. "I found something."

"What?"

She scooted closer to him and tucked under his arm. When she was feeling insecure, she'd cuddle close and talk quietly. "I found a duplicate code on his hard drive."

"And what does that usually mean?"

"It doesn't. I mean, you have code that runs the programs and orders the information in the programs. Having an exact duplicate set of code for one hard drive is useless and redundant." She sighed again. "Vista was methodical and intentional. This wouldn't have just happened unintentionally."

Zane pulled her into his lap and held her close, his chin resting on the top of her head. "So, you need to investigate."

"Yeah." She groaned. "Only I have no idea where to start."

"Well, is the code exactly the same?"

"Mostly, except for some extraneous letters and numbers."

"Do you have those?" Zane reached for her tablet and handed it to her.

"Yes, but you see a handful of letters and numbers." She called up the screen.

"A puzzle? A message perhaps?" He stared at

the jumble.

"That's what I think. Only I can't find any rhyme or reason for it. Taken out of context from the code it is nonsense; in the code, it just looks like stray keystrokes."

"But Vista wouldn't make that kind of mistake."

"No, he wouldn't. What am I going to do?" She looked up at him with her big green eyes.

"You are going to let your beautiful brain work on it while we get to Aruba. I know you'll figure it out. We need to finish packing and then get to bed. We leave for the airport at five in the morning."

"The secure comms pallet should arrive in Aruba with the security detail today." She grabbed his neck when he moved to stand up with her in his lap. Her shriek of happiness and then outright laugh were the reason he did it. She loved it when he did the 'He-Man' thing. Her words, not his.

"Once we have that set up at Gabriel's location, you and I are going to do nothing but lay in the sand and drink fruity alcoholic drinks." Zane laughed and planted his feet as Jewell literally climbed his body and wrapped herself around him for a piggyback ride down the hall. She grabbed his earlobe in her teeth, tugging it for a split second before she released it and laughed.

"You do realize you just said we could drink bad stuff."

"Hey, fruit is not bad stuff." He'd make sure the drinks had more fresh fruit in them than liquor. He hitched her up a bit and started walking down the hall to their bedroom. He glanced at the clock. He had nothing else left to pack other than Jewell's computer and tablet, and that wouldn't take long. Jewell, on the other hand, had yet to put a stitch of clothing into the suitcase.

"What do you want to take?" He dropped her legs once they hit the bedroom.

She opened a drawer and swiped an armful of underwear and dumped it into her half. "Swimsuits, shorts, tops, and maybe a pair of pants."

"Sundresses? The family might have a dinner or something." He'd bought her several over the summer, but they'd found a home in the back of the closet. His woman had a style. Yoga pants and t-shirts at home and jeans and nicer tops at work.

He turned in time to watch her dump all the shorts and t-shirts from her bottom drawer. She put her hands on her hips and stared at the suitcase. "Flip-flops and hair ties." She spun and went into the bathroom, obviously going for the hair ties. He went to her closet and pulled several pairs of sandals and her favorite leather flip-flops out. The jumbled mess on her side of the suitcase was so like his wife. Things like what to wear were just not important. He'd righted most of the clothes by the time she came back, sans hair ties.

She stopped in the middle of the room and stared at him. He straightened and waited for her to formulate what she wanted to say. Actually, she was probably having the entire conversation in her head without consulting him. She turned and left the room again. He chuckled and continued to fold her t-shirts. Jewell stepped back into the room and asked, "When are we going to have children?"

Okay... Looking for hair ties led her to a conversation about children. He needed to understand how that happened. He dropped the shirt he was folding. "Jewell, do you want children?"

She stared at him, and then her brow furrowed. "I think so."

He shoved the suitcase to the side and sat down on the bed. He patted the mattress beside him and waited for her to come sit down beside him. "Okay, walk me through it, please."

She huffed and pointed to the bathroom. "I went to get hair ties and saw I had one of Tori's from this weekend." She stared up at him as if that answered everything.

"Right, so, did Tori say something about having children?"

"Yeah."

Bingo. God, he was getting downright good at following her logic. "What did she say?"

"She asked when everyone was going to have kids. I told her I didn't understand the way they are programmed, but everyone said that they just wing it and hope for the best. Even Joy wants to have a baby."

Zane blinked and snapped his mouth shut. *Moriah* wanted kids. Holy fucking hell. Stop the presses. That was a headline that would stun the Shadow world. He'd try to process that bit of information later. "Oh, okay. Well, first, I'd love to have children. I thought you were against it. We've had this conversation, remember?"

"Yeah, and you said it was up to me and that you wouldn't pressure me." Jewell nodded. "You're not pressuring me."

Zane blew out a lungful of air. "Okay. You realize you'd have to put in shorter hours if we started a family."

Jewell jumped up from the bed and started

pacing. "Yeah, I get that. That's okay. You have the right people in the right places in the section. I mean, we wouldn't be able to leave for two weeks for an unscheduled vacation if you didn't, right?"

He nodded and let her continue.

"As I see it, we have several cons. Children would require one of us to stay at home at all times or take them with us if we go to the ranch like Tori and Jacob do. Traveling together would be impossible, and I'm not sure I'm happy with that. However, I can do my job from my office and I don't really need to travel; others can go in my place. But I don't want to give up my job. Tori still works part-time, but I want to work full-time. I like what I do."

He nodded when she looked at him. She didn't need his input right now. She was working through the scenario she had in her head, and if he interrupted her, it could take weeks or months before the topic could come up again. He was very interested in knowing her thoughts on a family.

"The biggest con is that I would make a horrible mother." She linked her fingers behind her neck and stared at him.

"I don't believe that for a second."

She spread her hands out. "I *forget* to *eat*."

"You take excellent care of me," he countered.

"Huh?" She blinked at him.

"You take excellent care of me." He stood and walked to her so she was looking up at him.

She narrowed her eyes and asked, "How?"

"Babe, you schedule everything for me. I know what to do and when to do it because you make sure I know. I wouldn't be able to accomplish half of what I do if you didn't prep me for it and clear most of the obstacles before I even know they're there." He placed his hands on her waist.

"But that's work. That makes sense to me." She dropped her hands. "I don't know how to take care of a baby." She dropped her eyes and whispered, "But I want to hold our child in my arms."

Zane blinked at the honest, raw emotion. He tipped her chin up so he could see her eyes. "There are classes, all kinds of classes, and books where you can get information. Your mother raised eight children; she wouldn't let you fail. Tori lives on the other side of town, Faith is even closer. Sweetheart, you will be a fantastic mother, but there is help if we need it."

She dropped her eyes and nodded. He could imagine the gears in her mind making a shift to accept the additional information. "What are you thinking about?"

She shook herself slightly. "Ahh... we'll go to the classes and read the books. When I have enough information and I understand more, maybe then we can try to have a baby?"

"Absolutely. But for now, how about we just practice?"

Jewell flashed a fabulous smile at him. "We want a perfect baby, right?"

Zane slapped a serious expression on his face. "Of course. Absolutely perfect."

"Then we must practice." Jewell placed her hands on his shoulders and jumped up.

He caught her legs and bounced her higher, grabbing her under her ass. He strode into the bathroom and dropped her in the middle of the double vanity. Their kiss lasted until they were both breathless. Recovery comprised the time it took to open the shower door and turn on the water. Turning back to her, he unwrapped the layers of clothing from his woman. Somewhere under the hoodie, the sweater, t-shirt, leggings, and two pair of socks was the sexy body he wanted to touch. "How in the hell aren't you sweating buckets?" He pulled off the last sock and glanced at the pile of clothing she'd wrapped herself up with.

She shrugged. "I don't like being cold." She leaned forward and looked at him. "Take yours off." She reached behind her and unfastened her bra. He stayed kneeling in front of her, waiting for that piece of fabric to find the mound of castoff material, but she smiled and then laughed. "Not until I see some flesh."

He stood and moved between her legs, stripping out of his t-shirt as he rose. Her hands released her clasp, and she shrugged off the lace. The only thing that barred his way to a very naked wife was a wisp of fabric. He smiled at her and grabbed the material at both hips and––

"Damn it, Zane! They were a matched set." She groaned and picked at the fabric that no longer circled her waist.

"I'll buy you more." He shucked his sweats and grabbed her off the vanity.

"You always say that."

"I do, don't I?" He stepped into the shower and walked them directly under the water. "I'll be saying it when I'm ninety."

"I'll be a wrinkled old woman."

"You will always be sexy to me. Always." He

shut the shower door behind them and let her legs slide down his. Her mind was a thing of beauty, her body was sexy beyond belief, but it was her heart that won him over. He'd seen it bleed for so many people for so long, there was no doubt in his mind that she would make a fantastic mother.

CHAPTER 8

Drake carried Jillian's suitcase and stowed it in Gracie's underbelly. The old girl was going to get a flying workout in the next couple days, but she was a solid aircraft and they'd just had her overhauled last year.

Jillian waited for him at the stairs to the aircraft. "You know they are going to be late, right?"

Drake grabbed his wife's hand, and they boarded together. "Who? Keelee and Adam, Mike and Taty, or Dixon and Joy?"

"Your brother. I went to ask Joy if she was ready to go and by the sounds of the way the headboard was thumping against the wall, it could be quite a while."

Drake turned to look at her and laughed at the deep red blush on her face. "Jilly, you realize other people do what we do after dark, right?"

"I'm not a prude, it's just... Things you can't unsee even if you imagine them, you know?" She dropped into one of the leather loungers. "Did you know Joy wants to have a baby?"

"What?" Drake glanced around the empty plane as the echo of his shout died down.

"Yeah, that was the response of everyone at Maliki's wedding. She got really quiet and I think our shocked response... ah... hurt her feelings."

Drake sat down across from his wife and made a pained face. "It is quite possible that woman doesn't have feelings unless it involves Dixon."

"No, she does. She just hides them from everyone. But yeah, she said she wanted a baby." Jillian cleared her throat. "We've never really discussed children other than, you know, commenting that maybe, someday..."

Drake rubbed his face with both hands and blew out a stream of air. "Yeah, well, you know what a fucking bastard my father was."

She nodded. "So, you never want kids?"

"Ah, well..." Drake checked the open door to make sure there was no one around before he continued, "Honestly, I'd like to be a dad, but I don't want to *father* children."

Jillian blinked at him. "What?"

He leaned forward. "I know it is an irrational fear. My father was the worst kind of evil; my mother wasn't much better. I don't want those people's genetics to run through my children's veins. It terrifies me that in some cosmic genetic lottery our son or daughter might end up mentally ill like they were."

Jillian covered her hands with his. "I understand completely, and to be honest, I don't think I'd do well with an infant. I know my limitations, but I love older children. Their curiosity and the way they search for answers. I'm amazed at how easy they assimilate facts and adapt to novel ideas. I guess it's too bad we can't just skip the first couple years, yeah?" She chuckled and then snapped up. "Wait. We *could* adopt. There are a lot of older kids in the system."

"Adopt?" He drew back. Why had he never thought about adoption?

"Or foster. Or both. Could you love a child that wasn't yours?" She leaned forward, her eyes brilliant with unspoken emotion.

"God, Jilly, I really get a kick out of all the kids

here at the ranch. I mean, yeah, I think I could. What about you?"

She nodded, and tears formed in her eyes. "I remember Cliff when he took us in. He was impossible. He didn't know how to cook. He tried way too hard to get us to like him, but he was there for us. Every day, he got up, and he was there for us. When we were happy or sad or when we threw tantrums because we were lost and confused, he was right there. He never wavered. I know I could do that, that *we* could do that. We can be that person. We could be there for a child who needed someone."

"We'd need to clear it with Guardian. If need be, we can build a house in Hollister so the kids could have a stable life but still be segregated from the business side of Guardian." Drake smiled and leaned forward to kiss her.

When he pulled away, she whispered, "You'd be willing to leave Dixon and move off the ranch?"

"In a heartbeat. Dixon has a wife, and from what you're telling me, they may start working on a family. I'll always live close to him, but I don't need to live in the same house. We can start looking for house plans and a plot of land."

"Are you sure?" She put a hand on his cheek.

He stared into her beautiful, expressive eyes. "I'm positive. Let's research our options and find out what we need to do. I want a family with you."

He leaned back in for a kiss as he heard people laughing outside the aircraft. "Hold that thought."

She groaned. "All the way to Aruba?"

"No. Just to D.C. We're spending the night and then flying to Aruba." He lifted his eyebrows suggestively.

Jillian drew a deep breath. "Drake?"

He stood up and glanced at the three couples and one little girl walking toward the plane. "Yes?"

"Fly fast."

He groaned and palmed his hard cock, adjusting himself out of the view of the latecomers. It was going to be a *long* damn flight. He wondered how fast he could push Gracie. It was about time to find out.

∼

Jade King picked up a red bikini top and wrinkled her nose. The barely-there material would be okay in an adult-only setting, but her nieces and nephews would be running around. *Speaking of which...* She dropped the red suit and grabbed a one-piece navy blue suit with white stripes as she yelled, "We aren't going to do the beach." She tossed in two more one-piece suits and grumbled, "I get sand in places sand should never be." A stack of shorts and summery tops and a few nice dresses went in after the swimsuits. She leaned back and hollered, "I'm decreeing dibs and we are staking out chairs at the pool. I pity the person who tries to usurp me this time. I want that corner near the palm tree. That's where the alcohol is." She muttered the last part to herself. She loved her brothers' and sister's kids, but they made her nervous. How she got roped into saying she'd take a day with another couple to watch the older ones was beyond her. *Oh, right. Too many damn mimosas after their impromptu breakfast in Jazz's room.* "Hey, *we*, meaning *you*, are on tap to help with the kids one day in the next two weeks."

She sniggered to herself. Nic was great with kids; he'd have a blast. When there was no reply, she headed out to the family room. The huge sectional with magical cushions from heaven had cradled them to sleep too many times to count.

Well, that's why he didn't answer her. That damn game again. The newest zombie apocalyptic game was blazing across the projection screen. Nic was so engrossed that he didn't even acknowledge her when she stood beside him. Yes, *this* was her man-child. A massive explosion sent zombie pieces flying across the screen. *Gross.* She hip-checked him and he glanced up at her. He shouted, "I'm a god! I just completed level thirty-seven!"

She flinched and pushed off his headphones. "Holy hell, stop yelling. I've just gone deaf. You said we needed to pack."

"We are." He pushed some buttons on his controller and stood up. "I was just taking a break. We are officially on vacation and I'm going to enjoy every minute."

She sidled up to him and wrapped her arms around his waist. "It isn't fair that you started our vacation without me. I've been working."

His eyebrows rose, and a smile slid across his face. "I'm sorry. Should I make it up to you?"

"You know, DeMarco, you are still not the sharpest stick in the box, but you're learning."

She laughed when he grabbed her and tossed her onto the couch. He moved with a little more caution, lowering himself over her. "One of these years I'm going to get a complex."

"Damn it, man, I have to amp up my tactics if

this process is going to take years." She wiggled under him and pulled her t-shirt up over her head and flicked it across the room. "Pay your penance, lover. Fuck me like you mean it."

She tapped his arm, and he lifted it. Jade jumped off the couch, shed her jeans, bra, and panties and then kneed onto the couch and placed her forearms on the back of the couch. She looked over her shoulder and waggled her eyebrows. "Come and get me, big boy."

Nic stood and unbuttoned his shirt. Jade decided against waiting at the sight of those muscled arms and ripped abs. She scooted back, stood up, and spun. "Changed my mind." Her hands traveled over his chest, pushing his shirt off his shoulders. She leaned forward and licked, then nipped his nipple. His body jerked, and she smiled against his skin.

She loved the feel of his hands as they traveled over her body, stopping to tease sensitive places. She unfastened his belt buckle and shucked his slacks and boxers down over his hips. "Sit down, DeMarco, I'm about to make you lose your mind."

She waited until he sat down and spread his legs before she slid his slacks off him, careful to avoid his prosthesis. Once he was free of clothes, she ran her hands up the inside of his thighs and watched his cock kick. "Want something, DeMarco?"

"Only what I was promised." He shuffled his fingers through her hair, not holding her, just connecting them.

Well, she had better ways of connecting them. She leaned forward, placed a hand at the base of his cock, and lollipopped the head until her hand was slick with her efforts. She stroked him and did her best Hoover impression, sucking the head of his cock into her mouth. His hips jerked upward, and his hands tightened in her hair. If she could have smiled, she would have, but that would have interrupted her fun. She popped off him and stroked his shaft several times before she lowered and nuzzled his balls. She took one into her mouth. Nic's legs trembled as they tightened around her. She released him and moved to the other side, giving him equal attention before returning to his shaft and deep-throating him.

"Fuck! Jade, I'm close."

She released him and wiped her mouth with the back of her hand while eyeing him. "On your back."

Nic scooted further onto the couch and held

her waist as she mounted him. He held his cock, and she lowered herself onto his shaft. His hands found her breasts, and he rolled her nipples between his fingers. She lifted her hair off her shoulders and let it flow around her arms as she lifted and lowered on his shaft.

Nic lowered one hand and she purred, knowing what was coming next. His thumb found her clit, and he matched her pace, pushing her closer to her own climax. She dropped her arms onto his chest and stared into his eyes as she changed her tempo, moving from teasing both of them to getting what they both wanted. She rocked up and down on him, grinding just a bit at the bottom, stimulating herself against his body. He grabbed her waist, and she knew it was only a matter of time before…

Like magic, Nic knew when she couldn't maintain the pace any longer, when her desire and need overcame her ability to keep moving. He held her in position and took over, claiming her as fast and as hard as she had been riding him. It didn't take long. Nic knew how to catapult her over the edge, and she flew past that ridge like a fucking rocket.

She collapsed on top of him and held him as he found his release. Once they both caught their breath, she rolled off him onto the couch beside him. The soft leather was cold on her back, but damn it, she wasn't going to move for a while. She drew a deep breath and then fidgeted. *Ok, maybe she was going to move. Itchy wasn't conducive to post-orgasmic bliss.* She pulled her hair out from behind her back and flopped it away from her. "Is it crazy that I'm looking forward to two weeks with my family, but I don't want to be with them all the time?"

"No. Besides, Joseph's place is huge, and we can play tourist on the island. We only have to be as social as we want to be." Nic rolled so he was facing her.

"Yeah, I'm not sure about that. You know how things happen—they make grand plans and we're dragged into them."

Nic chuckled. "Like how you planned our wedding and made every one of your brothers and sisters help?"

Jade narrowed her eyes and rolled to face her husband. "Yeah, like that. Watch it, DeMarco, or you'll end up in the doghouse before we even leave for Aruba."

"Isn't that my permanent residence?" He laughed when she swatted his arm. Nic enfolded her into a hug and kissed her forehead. "Your family is a mess, but they're wonderful. We'll have a great time. Zane was talking about maybe having a guys' day out or maybe doing some deep-sea fishing."

Jade tipped her head back to look at him. "Will that be okay with the roll and the pitch of the boat?" His stride was almost perfect. No one would know he had a prosthesis, but sometimes his equilibrium played hell with him and that was because of the percussion of the explosion. An inner ear imbalance that they hadn't been able to correct.

"I think so, and if I plant my ass in a chair all day, that is fine, too."

"Oh, by the way, you're babysitting with me when we go to Aruba. We are on the hook for one day out of fourteen, so if that deep-sea fishing thingy happens on the day we get stuck with watching the kids, you're staying on dry ground, copy?"

Nic lifted on his elbow and stared at her. "You volunteered to watch the kids?"

Jade snorted and rolled her eyes. "They forced me into it. Mob mentality is alive and well, along with one too many mimosas. We're taking turns so the people who brought the little buggers into the world can make more of them."

"Well, practice makes perfect. Joseph and Ember are expecting again. That's cool." Nic smiled and bent down to kiss her.

When he lifted away, she pushed out the question before she could stop herself. "Are you upset that I don't want kids?"

"What?" Nic blinked and then shook his head. "No. Why would you think I was?"

She leaned up on her elbow, too. "Because you like kids and I know you wanted a big family before we got married and I'm the one that just made the unilateral decision not to have any and--"

"Whoa, stop right there. Damn, you got yourself all worked up over this, didn't you?" He pushed her hair out of her face and cupped her cheek. His warm hand grounded her to him, slowing the tornado of thoughts whirring around in her mind. "How long has this been bothering you?"

She shrugged. "A while. But at Mal's wedding, when you and the rest of the guys were dying, the Coven had breakfast."

"I seem to recall something about that. Barely."

Jade laughed in spite of herself. Her husband wasn't a big drinker, and when he spent time with her brothers, they all paid for being stupid in public.

"We found out Ember was pregnant and the conversation just kind of grew along those lines. Everyone was open to having kids or *more* kids except me." She sighed and dropped her head against his chest.

"Everyone? Really?" He carded his fingers through her hair and tugged it a little when she didn't answer.

Finally, she nodded. "Joy said she wants a kid. Joy! That shocked the fuck out of all of us." She sighed and shook her head. "I feel like I *should* want them, but I don't. You really got a prize when you married me, DeMarco."

"First off, I knew exactly who I was marrying. I didn't marry you to change your mind or make you a different person. You are who you are, and I am who I am. Hell, you don't try to stop me from playing my stupid zombie games or coddle me when we do our training or rehab, and woman, you know I wouldn't put limits on you. That's not who we are. I accepted when we got married that it was going to be us and only us, and I am more than okay with that. We have nieces and nephews and by the sounds of it at *least* one more on the way. Children don't *fulfill* a person, babe. They make a life fuller. Our life is full to the brim with the love we share. Not having kids is our prerogative, just like having a family is theirs. They don't live our life. They don't get a vote."

Oh, damn, he understood. She knew he did, but she needed to hear it. She had to make sure she wasn't being a selfish bitch. His words wiped away the worries that had been plaguing her since Mal and Poet's wedding. She swiped at the tears that formed. "Damn it, DeMarco, that squishy inside you have showed up again."

She pressed close to him when he folded her back into his arms. "Yeah, I know. I'll have to work on that."

"Make sure you do." She sniffed and then smiled as his chuckle vibrated through her. "I fucking love you."

He kissed the top of her head and spoke quietly, "I know, babe. I love you, too."

CHAPTER 9

"What did you do? They're quiet as church mice." Anna handed Amanda a cup of hot peppermint tea as she sat down.

"I gave them all new coloring books and colors. The older boys got coloring pencils. They'll be good for at least a half-hour, and by then, Jacob will be here." Amanda took a sip of her tea. Her eyes popped open. "Oh, you spiked the tea!"

Anna chuckled. "I found something I like as much as cold red wine. Peppermint schnapps in hot peppermint tea. The young woman buried somewhere inside this old body tried it when my youngest daughter was home for Thanksgiving and made the rest of the brood a batch. It's good, isn't it?"

"No, darlin', this is fantastic." Amanda took another sip and closed her eyes. "Warms the bones and delights the soul."

"Where is Jacob anyway? I thought everyone was leaving work early today to get ready for the trip." Anna smiled at Gabriel and Frank when they walked into the living area of the hotel suite.

"He is taking the dogs to a lady who will watch them." Frank lowered himself onto the couch where Amanda sat.

"Where have you two been? We are on vacation."

"Does your vacation entail watching your grandchildren?" Gabriel sat down next to Anna and sniffed. "Ah, after the schnapps again?"

Anna elbowed him and laughed. "Vacation, remember?"

"My grandbabies are a delight and I'd gladly spend the entire two weeks watching them, but Tori told me that the couples are going to take a day each with the older kids so everyone can enjoy their vacation. Now, where did you two get to?"

"Joseph called. He wanted to inform us about an event happening in the near future. Some things you can't delay and must address when called." Gabriel lifted an eyebrow and Frank smirked.

"Oh, no. I've seen that look." Amanda turned to face her husband. "Frank Marshall, the last time I saw you make that face the kids ended up with puppies for Christmas."

Frank grunted but added, "Teaches them how to be responsible."

Anna cocked her head. "Really? Aren't some of the children too young to deal with the responsibility of a puppy."

Frank shrugged. "Wasn't talking about the *grand*children."

"I think the kids are doing very well for themselves. Chance and Elizabeth would have been proud of each of them." Amanda patted Frank on the leg.

Frank smiled at his wife and kissed her temple. "They turned out okay. Just need to keep them humble."

Gabriel snorted. "We finally have all four of ours settled. Deacon and Ronan aren't going to re-up. They're ready to come work for the business. They need to find a path forward. Gabriella settled in New York. She's changed career paths three times, but she finally decided on interior design.

She's a junior partner now, but when she's comfortable, we'll help her start her own company."

"What about the youngest? She's rather like our Jade." Amanda took another sip of her tea. "Delicious."

"Charlotte has an apartment in Paris. Believe it or not, my wild child is doing an internship on art restoration. She's a year and a half into a five-year program."

"Wow, that's an about-face for her, isn't it?" Amanda handed her teacup to Frank. "Try this."

Anna chuckled and pointed at her husband. "He didn't believe that his daughter could settle down." She narrowed her eyes at Gabriel. "He sent a team over there to watch her, to make sure she was where she said she was."

"Having a security company comes in handy," Gabriel admitted.

"Well, I think it's wonderful that she's settled." Anna patted Gabriel's leg. "And I'm especially happy that Daddy is finally trusting her to run her own life. She is twenty-one, dear."

"Doesn't make a difference." Frank shook his head. "A father needs to keep tabs on his children. I'd hate to think what would have happened to Tori if I hadn't stuck my nose into her business."

"I'm glad we could help with that situation." Gabriel's grave response earned him a nod from Frank.

Anna glanced from one man to the next. "What? What did you do for Tori?" She swung her attention to Amanda. "Do you know?"

Amanda shook her head. "No. I have no idea what they are talking about."

"Tori had an incident when she was working for the C.I.A. I asked Gabriel to check things out behind the scenes. He helped." He patted Amanda's leg. "She doesn't know and I don't think we need to tell her. Everything worked out well enough." Frank took a sip of the tea and recoiled, handing it back to her. "I'd prefer bourbon or a single malt Scotch."

"I can help with that." Gabriel stood and headed over to the bar. He leaned out so he could see into the other room and smiled. "They're having fun, no bloodletting yet."

"They do have their moments, but Talon, Reece, Blake, and the twins are great with Tristin. Lizzy mothers Chloe like crazy, but since they don't get in until later the boys are having fun together." Anna shrugged. "I raised eight kids, watching grandbabies for a few hours is child's play. Literally." She chuckled and sipped her tea. She winked at Anna. "I don't care what he says, this is amazing."

"I don't know how you did it. I raised four, and they wore me to a frazzle some days." Anna took another sip of her tea as Gabriel delivered a drink to Frank and sat down beside her with his.

Amanda sighed. "Well, you do what you have to do. I could never make ends meet if Chance didn't have the insurance policy from Guardian. That money allowed me to stay at home full-time until they were older. It worked, although their father's death was hard on each of them. Lord, there were days when all I did was cry, but I wiped away those tears when the kids came home from school. They needed a parent who was there for them. I gutted out the first couple years. As the kids grew, it became easier. Chance had a couple brothers who reached out and offered help. They were there if I needed them, and we visited a couple times, but driving from Mississippi to the upper East Coast is one heck of a trip. They had jobs; we had a life down south."

"I understand doing what you have to do."

Anna's eyes traveled to her husband. They'd had a rough start. The urgency of taking care of their unborn baby had driven her into hiding and away from the man she loved.

Gabriel nodded and wrapped an arm around her. "When Amanda contacted me after Joseph went after Chance's killer, we agreed that we would try to provide a career path for each of them with Guardian or one of the other businesses."

Amanda nodded. "The only one who wanted nothing to do with Guardian was Justin, but Gabriel was able to help him get into the restaurant business." She smiled at Gabriel. "You were literally our family's Guardian Angel."

Anna smiled. Her husband had been a helping hand to so many people, but these two and their family—she was very glad he'd taken a special interest in both of them.

Frank took a sip of his drink. *"That* is a drink." He winked at Amanda before he continued, "Got to admit it, Gabriel, you've been a friend to all of us when we needed you."

Gabriel drew a deep breath. "I made a promise to myself a long time ago. Doing what was right would never take a backseat to making money.

Taking care of my people and a decent business ethic is the hallmark of Guardian and now the other businesses I took over from my family. I have surrounded myself with people who believe in the same values, morals, and ethics. I made the mistake of overlooking character flaws once before, and it almost cost me my wife and future."

Anna placed her cup on the end table and tucked closer to Gabriel. "Where did you first meet Gabriel, Frank?"

"Huh…" He rubbed his chin. "San Diego, in passing when I was in the Navy. Then again in Libya before I ran into him in Bolivia."

"That's where I *finally* convinced him to come to work for me." Gabriel laughed. "He was a cantankerous country boy even back then."

Anna snorted. "I believe there is a lot more to that story."

Frank grunted. "Maybe a bit."

A loud knock sent all the kids scurrying to the door. "Whoa there!" Frank bellowed the command, and every child froze in their tracks. "Who opens the door?"

Talon's shoulders dropped. "An adult. But Grandpa, I was going to ask who it was first."

"Nope, you know the rules. An adult opens the

door. I don't care whose house, mine or yours, doesn't matter––an adult always answers the door."

"But Grampa, didn't the team check them?" Reece looked from the door to Frank.

"We won't always have security around, Reece. It is always best to be safe," Amanda said. "Children, back to the table. We have to pick up our things, that should be your ride to your sleepover."

Frank glanced out the peephole and opened the door. Jacob and Jared stepped into the luxurious presidential suite Gabriel had procured for both couples.

"Get the animals tended to?" Frank closed the door behind the two men.

"Yes sir. Are you ready for us to relieve you of the horde?" Jacob bent down and hugged Tristan and Tanner, who'd escaped clean-up duty. "Hey dudes, did you have a good time with Grandma and Grandpa?"

"Yes sir," they said in unison.

Jacob stood with a boy in each arm. "Were they good?"

"Perfect angels," Amanda called from the table where the older boys were hurriedly putting away the coloring books, crayons, and colored pencils.

"Where is your man?" Frank asked Jared.

"At home. He's putting Marcus to bed, and he has a video call with the manager of the shelter to make sure nothing drops through the cracks. He'll probably need to sit in on a couple meetings via video from Aruba. Are we going to have that capability?"

Gabriel nodded. "Full comm set up, and unless there is an emergency, Jewell is not authorized within a hundred feet of the door."

"Good luck with that." Jared chuckled. "There's the crew!"

"Hey, Uncle Jared!" Talon gave his uncle a high five and the younger boys followed suit.

"All right. Two cars. Blake, Reece, Talon with me, the twins and Tristin with your dad. Where's your coats?"

"Here." Anna held up two armfuls of coats, hats, and gloves. With adult help, the kids were bundled in record time.

"See you at the airport at eight?" Jacob asked before he opened the door.

Gabriel laughed, "No, we're taking my jet down later. We'll call when we get to the villa we rented."

"Perfect. Chad and Jasmine are flying down and bringing Jade, Nic, Jewell, and Zane. We've got a full load with the ones flying in from South Dakota. We will see you in Aruba."

"Be safe and be good for your dad and uncle." Amanda blew a kiss at the boys.

"We will!" the boys promised as they scurried out the door.

Anna waited until the door shut before she turned on her husband. "I thought we were leaving first thing in the morning."

"Ah, well, we were, but Frank and I need to pick up a few things before we head down." Gabriel put his arm on her waist and guided her back to the small lounge they'd been in before Jacob and Jared arrived.

"What aren't you telling us?" Anna stopped and narrowed her eyes at him.

"Nothing that you need to worry about, I promise." He leaned down and kissed her.

"Uh-huh." She glanced over at Amanda. "Are you buying this?"

"Not for a second." Amanda crossed her arms and looked at Frank.

He lifted his hands. "If you want me to ruin the surprise…"

"A surprise?" Anna whipped around and grabbed her husband's arm. "What?"

"No way, sweetheart. I'm keeping this secret under penalty of being skinned alive." Gabriel laughed and avoided her attempt at a swipe at him. He wrapped her in his arms. "How about we brew some more peppermint tea and order up some food?"

"Deal, but we are playing canasta. Amanda and I need to redeem our champion status."

Frank snorted, which earned him a look from his wife. "Oh, it is on Frank Marshall. We need two decks of cards."

Anna smiled as Gabriel went to order food and Frank and Amanda went in search of the cards. It occurred to her that life was a wonderful tapestry woven with colors of trial, friendship, love, and loss. Her tapestry was majestic and rich beyond her wildest dreams, but the brilliant threads she treasured most in that sweeping brocade were those of family and friends.

CHAPTER 10

"Wow." Jillian gasped as Drake walked with her out to the pool area of Joseph's massive estate in Aruba. Twinkle lights wrapped around palm trees and draped artfully overhead. The ocean rolled onto the beach beyond the pool area, highlighted by sweeping colors of rose, copper, and peach of the setting sun. "Have you ever seen anything this beautiful?"

Drake turned to her and folded her into his arms. "Every time I look at you."

She smiled and stood on her toes to kiss him. "That earned you brownie points."

"Oh, there's Christian. I wanted to ask him about possibly installing solar panels on the shelter and the community center to help eliminate some recurring monthly costs. Be right back." She pulled him down and kissed him quickly before she zeroed in on Christian and made a beeline in his direction.

Drake wandered over to the bar and watched as the bartender poured him a bourbon. Joseph had gone overboard tonight. He glanced to his right. A massive, thirty-foot-long table adorned in white linen and dotted with flowers, place settings, and yup, even name cards stood waiting for dinner. There was music playing softly through speakers camouflaged with landscaping around the pool. He wandered with his drink to the edge of the deck and glanced out to the ocean. So much had changed since he'd last been here. He glanced up at the massive residence. This was where Jason had asked Dixon to take on the assignment that separated them—in more ways than one. He'd left his brother and found Jillian. Dixon had found Joy. They'd come back together, yet the dynamics had shifted. Not worse or better, just different. He had his priorities and Dixon had his own. *Children. Wow.*

"Remember the last time we were here?" Mike stepped up beside him, his snifter of uber-expensive cognac in his hand.

PROMISES

"I do. It was a turning point." Drake took a drink of his bourbon.

"A curve on life's path. It took you to Jillian and Dixon to Joy." Mike swirled the amber liquid and stared at the waves.

"Makes you wonder what's next, doesn't it? Where we'll be the next time we're here?"

Chief chuckled. "That supposes we'll be invited again. I believe that our host was hoodwinked into the invitation."

Drake snorted. "Yeah, but two weeks in paradise. When was the last time we spent two weeks together? All of us?"

"Well… for the five of us on the old Alpha team, I believe it was at the ranch before that mission that went to hell."

"Damn, that's right." They'd reunited for other missions. The Maldives, where Mike and Taty were working undercover, then to D.C. when Dixon needed extraction.

Zane meandered over. "The last time I was here, I got married." He smiled. "Best fucking day of my life."

A waiter swooped by with a tray of appetizers. "Damn, Joseph went all out, didn't he?" Zane grabbed a napkin and two of the small offerings.

"Which raises a question." Jacob walked up with his drink.

"What's that?" Zane popped a shrimp-topped cracker into his mouth.

"How's he going to make us pay for this?"

"Hmm?" Zane's mouth was full, but he got his question across.

"Joseph has a plan." Jacob swung his eyes over to where his oldest brother was talking with Frank and their mom.

"You know that for a fact?" Mike took a sip of his cognac and sent a covert glance Joseph's way.

Jacob nodded. "You can bet on it."

Zane chuckled. "Well, we're fortunate that he has retired from his previous career. So, between the men and women who are here, everything else is manageable, right?"

Drake snorted. "You'd hope. But it seems he's fallen into his role as host." He nodded at Ember and Joseph as they moved from group to group and visited.

"I don't trust it. When was the last time you saw him this happy and this social?" Jacob glanced at Drake. "Be on your guard. He'll spring it when we least expect it."

"Roger that, Skipper."

Mike nodded and glanced around the growing gathering. "I concur. Where are Dixon and Doc? We need to advise them, too."

Zane tossed his napkin into a trash bin at the edge of the deck. "He's working this like a mission, isn't he? Damn it. He has something up his sleeve. I'll find Nic and Jared. I doubt Chad would be part of the payback, but I'll give him a heads-up just in case."

Jacob put a hand on Zane's arm, stilling him. "I'll let Justin and Jason know, too. Drake, you inform Dixon. Chief, you've got Doc."

"Roger that." The men echoed the affirmation and casually strolled away from each other.

∽

Joseph knew when the group in the corner broke up and he tracked them as they made their way through the crowd. Their surreptitious warnings would have been missed by someone who wasn't trained or, for that matter, currently training people on covert operations. He wrapped his arm around Ember's waist as she chatted with Anna. An added benefit to the plans he initiated. Being on alert the entire vacation for retribution that would come, but not in a way they would ever anticipate. Fools. Fuck around with a sharp knife and there was no doubt you'd get cut. Oh, he'd make them bleed, but not the red stuff in their veins. Nope, they'd be jumping through hoops.

Gabriel cleared his throat, bringing Joseph's attention back to him. "Thanks for the heads-up on that... operation. We took care of business this morning."

Joseph nodded his head. "Good." He glanced at the women as they held an animated conversation. Gabriel nodded to the corner. Joseph kissed Ember's temple. "Be right back."

She glanced at him and smiled. "Okay."

He and Gabriel moved out of earshot. "You know they know something's up."

Joseph's low, evil chuckle confirmed that he in fact knew.

"When are you going to tell them?"

"Tonight at dinner I'm going to tell them I have a private yacht hired for a day of deep-sea fishing. I'll drop *the* bomb when I have them as a captive audience. We will dock exactly twenty-four hours before the event."

Gabriel frowned. "They'll be able to find what they need." He lifted his drink to his lips.

"I don't doubt it. However, that day there will be four cruise ships docking at dawn."

Gabriel coughed, choking on his drink. Joseph patted him on his back until he could breathe. He accepted a napkin from a passing waiter and wiped his mouth. "You are one devious son of a bitch."

"They wanted to wedge their way into my vacation. Seems only appropriate that they experience *everything* with me. Right?"

"And the ladies?"

"I have that covered. It cost a fucking fortune, but I have everything in place. I swore you and Frank to secrecy."

Gabriel gave a firm nod before agreeing, "You have our word."

"I do, and for that, I thank you. Now, if you'll excuse me, I need to go be social and happy."

"Fuck, you're going to scare them to death before you run them to death, aren't you?"

"Oh, yeah." He laughed again. Maybe this vacation had potential after all.

Joseph tapped his spoon against his wineglass, stilling the babble of conversation around the table. "Thank you all for coming to Aruba on such short notice." There was laughter and clapping from the women and children. The men smiled but glanced around at each other. "I know everyone has plans, but I wanted to let you know that I'm giving most of my Christmas presents early this year. First, gentlemen, we have a full day on a luxury yacht, deep-sea fishing on the tenth. Ladies, I've hired the services of a local spa for you on that day. Hair, nails, facials, massages, the works. My staff has arranged to take the older children on ATV rides around the island with a picnic lunch at one of the beaches. The younger ones will have childcare here at the house." He glanced down the table to where the children were sitting. "Don't worry, many, many more presents will come on Christmas morning."

A loud happy choir of voices rose, and he lifted a glass of wine, speaking above the din. "A toast to family, by blood or by choice."

Everyone lifted their glasses in unison. Joseph took a sip and sat down, smiling at Jacob, who stared at him. Damn, he could see the wheels working in the little man's brain. He was having *fun* with this payback.

"What a wonderful gesture. I really thought you'd be upset that they came down." Ember leaned over and kissed him on the cheek.

"No, actually, I am enjoying having everyone here." He covered her hand with his. "Don't tell a soul that I just admitted that."

Ember laughed and smiled at him. "Your secret is safe with me."

CHAPTER 11

Jasmine watched her husband as he sang. The meal finished and children put to sleep, most of the adults had congregated on the beautiful balcony of Joseph's home. Her family enticed Chad to sing a couple songs, which he was happy to oblige. As the last notes of a haunting new melody faded, a warm and peaceful mood seemed to settle around the couples.

Jade leaned against Nic. "Hey, Jazz, do you ever miss being a PSO?"

She shook her head, her answer immediate. "Not at all. I mean, it was an exceptional experience, and it gave me Chad, but being in charge of his and our security is a full-time job. We've got a world tour coming up. Limited stops, but still enough to keep me more than busy. I've found my place in life and I couldn't be happier." She smiled at Chad, who dropped his arm around her and kissed her temple.

"Guardian has changed, hasn't it?" Jewell sighed. "Big changes, fast growth, exponential potential."

"It has," Jason agreed from across the balcony.

"Jason, where do you see Guardian in the next ten or twenty years?" Justin asked from where he and Dani were sitting by the railing.

Jason blew out a lungful of air and took Faith's hand in his. "Well, with twenty-six Alpha teams and thirty Dagger teams now trained and through the Rose, I'd say we are as big as we are going to get for the foreseeable future. Training at the Rose and at the complex will continue. The rehab center at the complex is as big as it is going to get, and we are going to work on building up the Rose for those who need long-term medical and mental health care. Of course, our Dom Ops side continues to grow as clients seek us out to ask us to investigate more. So, in twenty years, I imagine I'll hand the reins over to one of Gabriel's children, or perhaps one of ours, and they will take it into the next generation."

"It has been a spectacular ride up to this point, hasn't it?" Jacob asked to nobody and everyone. Heads nodded up and down.

"Hey, Skipper, I'm damn glad you showed up for that date with Tori, aren't you?"

Laughter erupted. "Oh, hell yeah. If she didn't show, I would have found her. Somehow. It was meant to be." Tori was sitting in Jacob's lap. She twisted and kissed him, whispering something quietly to him.

"Who would have imagined Guardian being such a huge part in all of our lives?" Jasmine chuckled. "Even Justin."

"A high-class thief," Dixon threw out.

"Cat burglar," Drake added.

"Information Extraction Specialist," Justin and Dani said at the same time, causing another round of laughter.

"Dude, you shocked the shit out of all of us," Jared chuckled.

Justin flipped his brother the finger, getting another round of laughter for his efforts. "For all the shit I get, I'd rather you still didn't know."

"Was that your choice or the organization's?" Joy asked from the dark corner where she and Dixon were sitting.

"Both," Justin admitted. "Gabriel channeled my extreme thrill-seeking into a profession that provided me the outlet and kept me away from guns. Which I still hate."

Jillian reached out and high-fived Justin. "You and me both."

"His skill set is impressive and no matter what you call him, he is damn good at what he does." Joseph pushed his foot against the floor, setting the double rocking chair he and Ember shared into motion.

Everyone nodded in agreement. Faith cleared her throat. "What do you think about the children eventually joining Guardian?"

Tori shrugged. "That will be their call. It is a damn good organization, but the risks in the field? The mother in me says hell no. I don't know how Amanda dealt with it."

"She is a strong woman," Taty agreed and leaned into Mike. "Both her and Anna. They had to be."

"What do you think they are doing over at the other villa?" Jade asked. "You think they are letting their freak flag fly?"

Jewell clapped her hands over her ears. "Ew!"

Nic's head dropped back. "Please, stop!"

Jacob groaned, "Damn it, Jade!"

Jasmine shoved her twin. "Gross."

"What? They're old, not dead! Why wouldn't they get busy? We are all going to do the horizontal mamba every chance we get while we're here. Right?"

"Well, now that makes it awkward to go to the villa." Mike stood up and offered Taty his hand. "But we do need to go."

"You're our ride, so we need to bail, too." Dixon and Joy stood.

Jasmine leaned against Chad as each of the couples made their way to their rooms. Chad put his arm around her. "You're sure you don't miss Guardian?"

She turned to look at him. "I'm positive. I wouldn't change a thing about my life. You and Chloe are everything to me."

Chad lowered his lips to hers. "Have you told anyone yet?"

"No, we haven't been to the doctor."

"The home pregnancy test confirmed what we both knew."

Jasmine smiled. "And here I was trying to convince myself I had the flu."

"I knew. Your body was changing." He pulled

her against him. "You'll be seven months pregnant when we finish the overseas leg of the tour."

"I will be. But with you taking six months off between the overseas and U.S. dates, we can go home, I'll nest, and we can both relax before he or she arrives."

"Our mothers are going to be over the moon."

"Like you aren't?"

"I am. I think we should tell them."

"When?"

"I'll let the guys know on the fishing trip. You let the women know at your spa day."

"That's an awesome Christmas gift."

Chad nodded. "Hopefully, your brother doesn't sink the ship."

Jasmine chuckled. "Joseph wouldn't kill family. He might make you wish you were dead…"

"I was not in on the 'Take Over Joseph's Vacation' game." Chad chuckled and stood, grabbing his guitar with one hand and offering the other to her.

"And yet, here we are." She stood and chuckled when Chad sighed dramatically.

"Well, it isn't often we get to be with all your family at the same time. I thought it was an outstanding idea, especially since everyone said they could come down."

"Thank you."

"I'd do anything for you." He lifted his hand. "See, I'm holding the moon and the stars in my hand for you." Chad halted.

He hummed a tune and looked down at her. She smiled and nodded into the house. "Your notebook is in the bedroom." She held his hand as they walked through the maze of Joseph's home. She listened as the music quietly flowed from her man. She'd spend the night listening to him write the song that was growing in his mind. It never got old. Her husband's talent and ability amazed her. His love and devotion to his family had put his career firmly in second place, but his talent didn't know that. The songs and music flowed through his fingertips and filled their life. A perfect melody to accompany a lifetime together.

CHAPTER 12

"All right, he's almost out of time. Do you think it will be today?" Adam stood beside Jacob on the dock as they watched the others getting onto the yacht.

He shook his head. "What is he going to do? Blow up the boat? He's been the perfect host." Not that they'd seen much of each other except for the elaborate dinners that happened every night. Tori and he had full days without the kids. He'd made love to his wife slowly. Which, with four boys and busy lives, didn't happen as much as either of them would like. They'd decided to make time for long weekend getaways to reconnect and restoke the fires.

"That's what scares me."

Jacob snorted.

"Screw you, Skipper. I'm not stupid, that man has plans. He's going to get us back, I just don't know how. This is a nice boat."

"She's a ship." The voice from behind them spun them both.

"Dan?" Jacob stuck out his hand. "What the fuck are you doing in Aruba?"

"Well, Joseph is my boss." The dumb shit went without saying. Smoke clamped Jacob on the shoulder and laughed. "We're on downtime. Charley, my partner, helped me get her down here but flew out to New York to visit family. I'm making a run to the airport tomorrow night to retrieve my partner from the city that never sleeps."

"What have you been doing? You're no longer partnered with Sage?"

"Nope, he had to punch. Family issues. And I haven't been doing much, bumming around, getting a tan, waiting to take y'all out fishing. This is a friendly island. Love the people here. Has everyone boarded?" Smoke took off his hat and pushed his hair out of his face.

Adam blinked and did a double-take. "I think so... Hey, you know you look a hell of a lot like--"

"Yeah, I get that a lot." Smoke laughed and perched his cap back on his hair. "We have a full galley and I have the frozen drinks spinning. Let's get this party barge moving!" He strode down the dock and Adam looked from him to Jacob.

"That man is the spitting image of ––"

"Let it go, Doc." He slapped his best friend on the back. "Let's go fishing."

Dan Collins jumped onto the deck and whistled. "Okay, my new best friends, my name is Dan Collins, this ship is my baby. Here's the drill for the day. The tackle and gear are on the bottom level. I'll let you know when it's safe to drop a line. You don't need to cast. Just drop the line. Those hooks can cause a nasty scratch so be careful when you bait up. If you cross a line you move, the line you crossed doesn't. We are going after White Marlin, Kingfish, and Wahoo, but you might get bites from Sailfish on the tackle we have. If you snag a bite, let everyone know by yelling, *Fish on*. Everyone who has nothing on the line will clear out of your way. These fish are powerful and hard to land. All of you look in good enough shape, but if you tire out, let someone else reel them in for a while. They will fight and fight hard." He rubbed his hands together. "What else? Oh, latrines are through the main cabin to the right. Galley is on the other side of the main cabin to the left. Plenty of food for you to eat in there, but I'm not playing servant. I have beer, water, and soda in an ice chest downstairs and there are frozen mango and strawberry daiquiris in the machines on the main level. Believe me, the heat will sneak up on you. Remember, shade is your friend." He turned to Joseph. "I'll need someone to cast off when I get her fired up."

"I'll take the bowlines." Zane headed to the front of the ship.

"I've got the stern." Justin headed to the back of the craft.

"Well, look at that, an instant crew. Explore the boat, we'll be in fishing waters in about an hour." Dan laughed and headed up the ladder to what Jacob assumed was the bridge. He scanned the deck until he found his oldest brother. The sneer that crept across his face was enough to send a shiver of apprehension down his back.

"He is up to something," he said to Jason, who was standing next to him.

Jason grunted. "He can't blow up the boat."

"You sure about that?" Jacob asked as he headed down to the beer. It may be early, but if he was going to be blown to smithereens by his own brother, he was going to do it with a buzz on.

~

Joseph scanned the men on the deck of the ship. If he'd been forced to admit it to anyone, he'd have to acknowledge that today had been a total kick in the ass. Chief had caught the biggest Wahoo and both Dixon and Drake had landed a Kingfish, but the battle of the day was his. He'd snagged a sailfish and had reeled that bastard in all by himself. It took over two hours of give and take. They hauled him onto the deck, took a picture, and let the son of a bitch go. They released all the fish. They weren't going to eat them, so it was the right thing to do. As the men stowed their rigs, he cleared his throat. Every eye turned his direction. Even Dan Collins stopped talking, which hadn't happened all day.

"Thank you for inviting yourselves to my vacation. I've had a great time and I hope you have, too. Three more days left on the island. I know you've been wondering when—or if—I'd be taking a shot at you."

"Definitely when," Double D said together.

"Okay, stop that." Joseph pointed to them. "I was coming down here with Ember to renew our vows since we found out we're pregnant. So, knowing that you gentlemen would not want to be left out, I have included each of you in the vow ceremony. As I speak, the ladies are being hand-delivered invitations, which they believe are from their husbands, to renew their vows on the beach with Ember and me tomorrow night."

Chief crossed his arms and stared at Joseph. "How is this retribution?"

"Ah, well… I've purchased Ember a ring to give to her when we renew our vows. In addition, the invitation they received indicates you have done the same thing."

"What?" Dixon and Drake spoke in unison again.

"Again, stop that shit." Joseph smiled at each of them. "They have fittings for their dresses tomorrow. The children will have a part in the ceremony. Jared, Christian and you will renew your vows with the rest of us. If you don't do rings, that's on you, but you will both be on that beach. Understood?"

Christian nodded his head, and Jared chuckled. "Guess we can find rings, too."

He smiled at Christian, who nodded. "Yeah, I'd like that."

"So, what's the big deal?" Jacob put his hands on his hips. "This island has a Diamonds International on it. We walk in, point to what we want, and bingo, done."

Joseph shrugged. Tomorrow was Sunday and everything but the tourist stops would be closed. He'd also arranged to have Gracie and Gabriel's plane down for maintenance. Chad and Jasmine had rented a private charter to deliver them and pick them up. It would force the men to wade through literally thousands of tourists to get to the store. Getting to the counter would be impossible. He smiled. "Glad you have a plan, little man. Glad you have a plan." He nodded at Dan, who gave him a look like he'd gone insane, and they both headed to the bridge.

Smoke closed the bridge door. "You realize cruise boats are going to dock tomorrow morning."

"I do." Joseph sat down and put his feet up on the rail circling the counter.

"And it's Sunday."

"Yep."

Smoke chuckled and hit the button to lift

anchor. "Oh, shit. They have a celebrity with them. Dude, that's fucked up. That guy is a mega superstar in the music world. One person says his name and it will be mayhem."

Joseph snorted. "A minor inconvenience."

"Yeah, the same way a death sentence is minor. They'll be lucky to get out of there alive." Smoke sniggered and pushed the throttle forward. "Why are you being so nice?"

Joseph sighed and dropped his head back, staring at the ceiling. "I think I'm mellowing in my old age."

Smoke glanced at him and started laughing. He stared at his friend and then glared at him. Not *that* fucking funny.

~

The men huddled in a circle. "There's a catch." Jacob stared after Joseph. Jared crossed his arms and drew a deep breath. *Yeah, there probably was.*

"But what?" Chad rubbed the back of his neck.

"I don't know. This isn't a big issue. He dropped the announcement like it was something important, though," Justin agreed.

"It should be easy enough. We'll all meet at

Joseph's tomorrow about noon, head down to the port, and go buy the rings." Jared looked at everyone as he spoke.

"There is something else," Nic said from the chair where his ass had been planted. His inner ear imbalance was giving him hell, but he'd hung tough all day.

"Ember's pregnant, so he wouldn't do anything at the ceremony." Jason scrubbed his face. "So is Faith, by the way."

"And Jasmine," Chad added.

A round of congratulations, handshakes, and bear hugs happened before they all settled down again. The harbor grew closer as they stared out into the water. "You know, maybe he's mellowed in his old age," Jared suggested.

"Joseph?" Jacob's voice hit an octave no man's voice should ever hit.

"I stand corrected." He sat down beside Christian. "So, you're going to marry me again?"

"I will and I am," Christian laughed. "You've mellowed in *your* old age."

Jared lifted an eyebrow. "Is that right?"

Christian drew away and smiled. "That's right."

"Christian?" Jared leaned toward his husband.

"Yeah?" Christian answered.

"When we get to Joseph's… run."

He watched his husband's eyes dilate and heard the soft rush of air from his lungs. "Run fast."

Christian nodded and swallowed hard; his Adam's apple bobbed. "Yeah, I'll run, but you better be chasing me."

"No, I'll be catching you. You better make it to our room, or we'll be putting on a show."

Christian's breath caught. "Fuck."

Jared leaned in and growled, "Exactly."

CHAPTER 13

Dixon stared at the snarl of pedestrian traffic. "What the actual fuck? Cruise ships? He knew, didn't he? He fucking knew." The cars that had dropped them off had left, and they were on foot... in hostile territory.

All heads nodded north and south. Jacob swore, low and pissed off. "Yeah, the fucker knew, and he couldn't have planned it better. Dixon, how long would it take to get Gracie to Miami?"

Drake answered, "Not long, Skipper, but that's not the problem."

Jason turned toward him. "What is the problem?"

"Gabriel said he was going to have his pilots

ferry both planes back to undergo maintenance while we were here," Dixon replied.

"Well, *this* is a problem." Chad pulled his hat down farther and ducked his head. "Guys, if someone recognizes me, we're screwed."

Zane stepped in front of Chad, blocking him from view of some of the people who formed a wall-to-wall barrier between them and the store where they needed to be. "We can get you there."

"Yeah, and what happens when someone recognizes him in the store?" Nic asked. "You saw what the people at the restaurant did to him."

"They have private areas for big spenders. They have to. With all of us buying rings, they'll move us into one of the areas they have set up. Then it will be a matter of getting you back. The cars will pick us up here," Jason spoke as he moved so he was blocking Chad from another angle.

Jacob turned to face them. "Look, we have to do this, so from this point forward this is an op. Pure and simple. Chief, you take the point. Dixon, Drake, you flank us, Zane and Jason, you are on Chad like fucking glue, you are his last line of defense. Jared, you're with Christian, and Justin, you're with Nic—you are the roving blockers. If anyone seems too interested, you get in their way.

Adam and I have our six. The store is one klick away north by northeast. We've covered rougher territory with more at stake, but I've seen this guy's fans. They are feral. The LZ is hot, we have no weapons but our wit, and according to my wife, that won't get us far, but we don't have a choice. If we fail, Chad will become dog chow and our women will know we didn't have a hand in this event. I, for one, liked the thank-you sex I got last night." He glanced around. Dixon agreed. He'd obtained a nine-and-a-half last night. Even though his little assassin would never admit it, she dug the fact the rest of the women included her in the girly things.

There was a grumble of agreement as they took up their positions. Chief made sure everyone was ready and stepped off. The mass of humanity that filled the port area decried any personal space. They moved forward, splitting the crowd of people coming off the cruise ships. They pushed upstream against the flow of swimsuit-wearing, coconut-smelling, suntan lotion-slathered tourists. Everyone stared at them. Dixon huffed and elbowed past people who'd stopped in the middle of the street to take pictures. Of course, they would stare. Their sizes alone would make them a spectacle, but the fact they were parting the crowd and hiding a man at the center of their formation drew even more eyes. They turned the corner, and he drew a breath. He could see the damn sign. Thank God.

He saw a woman tap another's arm and point to Chad. Damn it. They had less than a block to go. "Chief." His one-word warning pushed them forward at a higher clip. Damn it. Joy wasn't much for bling, but he wanted to get her a ring to celebrate their decision to start a family. Something she could pass down to their grandchildren someday.

"Move." Jared pointed to the store, and they darted to the tan building with the dark brown awning. They walked into the interior store area as one person, bringing every store clerk's eyes to them. Mike walked up to the first employee he saw. "We need to see the manager immediately."

The woman blinked at him and swept her eyes past him to the men behind him. "One moment, please." She put the ring she was showing back in the display case and locked it.

"But I wanted that ring," a woman sputtered as the employee scooted behind the counter.

Mike glanced at the display and shook his head.

He looked the woman up and down and smiled slowly. "You'd look better in rose gold."

Fuck. Dixon fought his smile when he watched the woman melt under Mike's attention. Chief had game; he really did. Who would have known? The woman's hand went to her throat, and she smiled in a kind of shell shocked way. "Do you really think so?"

Mike nodded. "Absolutely."

The manager made her way to them. "Sir, may I be of assistance?" Chief leaned down and whispered in the woman's ear. Her eyes grew large, and she nodded. "But of course. Right this way."

"See, I told you, *that is Chad Nelson.*" The woman Dixon had noticed earlier pointed to Chad.

"Oh, shit." Chad crowded past Jason and followed Chief. Zane moved up to lead the way and Jason was glued to his back.

The rippling murmur that went through the crowd grew louder. Dixon was never so glad to be shoehorned into a small room with too many people. The manager turned to them and smiled. "Now, what can we help you with?" She sized them up the way a tailor sized up a suit.

"We each need to buy a ring," Jason explained.

"But of course. I will be glad to help. Who is first?"

Mike spoke. "Platinum band, oval stone, baguettes on either side in the first display case on the right. Sized to a size five, please."

The manager's eyes widened. "You've been looking at our collection. An excellent choice. One minute."

"How the fuck?" Jacob looked at Mike.

He shrugged. "It was the ring the woman was looking at. I liked it and I think Taty would, too."

∽

Seven hours later, Jacob was over the entire concept. Adam was the last to choose his ring, and it was being sized.

He motioned over the manager. "We need a way through the throng of people and back to where our cars are going to pick us up." He'd just called Tori and asked her to have the cars pick them up where they'd dropped them off.

She smiled at him. "Sir, there is hardly anyone out there. Three of the ships have already set sail, and the last is waiting on a tour that has obviously been delayed, or they'd be gone, too."

She opened the door of the room where they'd waited. "We'll close after we've finished sizing your friend's purchase." The employees in the outer area smiled. "But if I may, would Mr. Nelson be able to sign a few autographs and pose for pictures with my staff?"

"Absolutely." Chad gave one of his smiles and Jacob watched the woman melt. He went out into the store and did the whole meet-and-greet thing.

Jason moved over beside him. "I couldn't live that way. I had no idea it was so bad."

Jacob nodded. "He doesn't have much freedom. I think that's why he likes the family events. He can just be himself; he doesn't have to be 'on'."

Adam pocketed his ring, and they all meandered out to the front of the store. It took another ten minutes for Chad to satisfy all the selfie requests, and Christian took several group photos for people.

"I need a drink," Mike grumped from beside him.

"We all need a drink," Jason agreed. Jacob snapped his head around to his brother. Jason chuckled and shook his head. "Ginger ale. I'm fucking thirsty."

Jacob's heart slowed a bit. His brother was a

rock for the organization and under a lot of stress, but he'd made a meeting every day while on the island.

"Let's go." Chad rubbed his hands together and headed to the door. Zane caught up with him and dropped a hand on his shoulder. "Whoa there, partner, let me make sure we are clear."

Chad stopped and motioned to the door that the manager had unlocked and opened for them. Zane walked out, looked right and left, and then turned back to the crowd. "We are home-free."

"Thank God." Jacob breathed the words as they left the store. They'd been treated very well by the attentive staff, but damn it, Joseph was going to pay for that shit.

"You know," Jacob said loud enough so that the entire group could hear him. "He's going to have to pay for this."

"No." Adam shook his head. "I will not be looking over my shoulder for the rest of my life."

"No shit," Chad agreed. "Today was okay because the staff was amazing, but it could have gotten really ugly."

"I say let him have his revenge and leave it alone," Nic gave his two cents.

"I'd love to punch him in the face, but the smart play is to let it go," Zane concurred.

He glanced over at Dixon and Drake. They smiled and winked at him in complete unison. *Fuck, that was weird as shit.* Well, at least he could count on the Wonder Twins.

"I'm going to stay out of it. The vacation idea was great, but I'm not getting into a feud with Joseph. We will not win," Jason added.

"Not worth it," Chief interjected his opinion into the conversation.

"What he said." Jared pointed at Mike.

Christian nodded. "I'm with him." He pointed at his husband.

Jacob walked up to the waiting cars and opened the door. "I am very disappointed in all of you."

Jason chuckled. "Don't be stupid, Jacob. Your kids need a father."

Dixon and Drake shot each other a look. Dixon shot him a look. "Hey, Skipper?"

"Yeah?"

Drake shrugged, "We're out."

Jacob groaned. He got in the car and stared out the window. A smile spread across his face. Even with all the bullshit with the crowds, today had been fun. Hell, the entire vacation had been damn near perfect. Tomorrow they'd line the beach and reaffirm their promises. For the future, for their families, and for love that bound them to the women and man who made this crazy life worthwhile.

CHAPTER 14

F rank put his arm around Amanda. The sunset beach ceremony had been perfect. He watched as his grandchildren ran up and down the beach and the men and women he loved, his family, laughed and celebrated with champagne.

The vows they'd repeated were profound and fitting. Knowing Joseph had written them had made them emotional for everyone. The words he'd memorized along with all the others filtered through his mind.

Our love has grown every day. This ring symbolizes my promise to continue to love, honor, and cherish you. Time has only strengthened our union. I will be there for you, in good times and in bad. I vow to do whatever it takes for as long as it takes to fulfill my promise. My promise is forged by life, strengthened by your love, and made without reservation.

"Is this what Joseph told you and Gabriel about before we left?" Amanda leaned into him. A piece of her hair blew across her cheek.

He tucked the strand behind her ear and nodded. "Joseph arranged everything."

Amanda laid her head on his shoulder. "That is quite the sight."

Frank chuckled at the words. He'd said the same thing many years ago when he first watched the family gather for Talon's christening. "We have an incredible family."

Amanda lifted her head and smiled up at him. "But they're still a handful, aren't they?"

He laughed, "God, yes."

Gabriel and Anna moved over beside them. "Look." He pointed toward Dixon, Drake, and Jacob.

"Oh, no." Amanda shook her head. "Will they ever grow up?"

"God, I hope not. This is going to be fun." Anna's hand covered her mouth, and she laughed.

"Oh, no. Jade's in on it," Gabriel chuckled.

Jade pulled Ember away from Joseph, pointing the opposite direction from where Dixon, Drake, and Jacob were coming from. Instinct must have clicked in, but Joseph was a second too late. All three men grabbed Joseph and carried him into the surf.

"I think the idea was to get Joseph wet," Amanda laughed as Joseph dunked Jacob. A shouted whoop came from Jade, who tackled Dixon and sent him into the water. Jared took down Drake and then all the grandchildren flung themselves into the water. Jason gave a war cry and ran into the surf with Reece on his shoulders.

Frank laughed until tears formed. Gabriel brought a hand down on his shoulder. "I've said it before, but those men and women are our nation's future. I couldn't imagine how the world would look without them."

Jewell and Zane walked up to them. Jewell carried her laptop clenched to her chest. "I'm sorry for interrupting. I hate to bring up work when everyone is so happy, but I think I found out what was on Vista's hard drive."

Gabriel looked at Frank, and they excused themselves from their wives. They moved over to the corner of the deck. "Go ahead."

Jewell cleared her throat and opened the tablet. "There were extra letters and numbers in the duplicate code. Vista got more information than we thought, but I don't think we were his only data-mine because he wouldn't have gotten this. Not from us. I'm not sure if this is the truth or if the bastard is playing games with us from the grave."

"Explain that for them." Zane put his hand on her arm. Whatever she'd found had rattled her. Frank watched as his daughter's hand trembled so badly she clenched her fist.

"Gabriel, I wouldn't know the significance of this if I didn't work this case for you years ago." She cleared her throat and showed them a screen with random numbers. "I made a program to put the letters into words and then form the most logical sentence from those words. It came up with thousands of sentences, most gibberish, but this made my heart stop." She pushed the space bar and the following words appeared.

LORI BAKER ENGINEER

Both he and Gabriel recoiled. "The numbers?" Gabriel shot the question out quickly.

"They *could* be longitude and latitude. The variables, when using them in random order, put them all over the globe. I'd need to get back to my office and go through a process of elimination."

"What is the likelihood that Stratus has this information?"

"If they have the disk, they have the information. Would they go into the code? I didn't. Not for years." Jewell's eyes brimmed with tears. "If she's alive, why hasn't she reached out?" Zane wrapped his arm around her waist.

Gabriel drew a deep breath and slowly released it. "If she didn't, it means she couldn't." He smiled down at Jewell. "You did a fantastic job. We'll work on this when we get back. This is higher than your brothers' and sister's clearance. They don't need to know. I'll brief Jason. Go have a drink and relax. Enjoy the rest of your vacation because you'll be busy when you get back."

Jewell lowered her gaze and closed her notebook. "I should have looked sooner."

"You can't worry about the past." Frank smiled at her. "It gets you nowhere. Kinda like pitching back and forth in a rocking chair. You're moving, but you're not going to get anywhere or do nothing but burn energy."

Jewell chuckled. "Have I told you lately how much I love you?" She smiled up at him.

"Not lately." Frank leaned down and kissed her cheek. "Now get. Go jump in the surf with the rest of those idiots."

Zane gave him a look. "The *rest* of the idiots?"

Frank grunted. "Caught that, did you?"

Zane laughed and shook his head. "Yes sir, I did." He smiled down at Jewell. "Come on, babe. We're done for tonight."

He watched as the couple sauntered away. "He takes damn good care of her."

Gabriel nodded. "That he does."

Frank reached into his pocket and withdrew two pieces of hard candy. "Taffy melts down here." He handed one to Gabriel and unwrapped the other.

"John said he watched the car blow up with her in it." Gabriel slowly unwrapped the candy.

"If she survived and someone found out who she was, it could be disastrous." Frank popped the candy into his mouth. He always found it easier to think when he had a bit of sugar.

Gabriel grunted in agreement. "My dilemma is do I tell him before we investigate?"

"I'd want to know." The man was going to be beside himself.

"I would too. You're heading back to the ranch after this, right?"

"I am." Frank nodded his head. "I'll tell him."

"Our country has screwed that man," Gabriel sighed. "God help me, I hope she's alive. For John's sake."

Frank nodded. Life had a way of twisting and turning. He watched his family laughing and splashing in the water as the sun threw the last brilliant rays of the day. "We made him a promise."

"We'll keep it." Gabriel nodded. "Unless he walks away from our protection, the world will never know that John Smith is still alive."

To read John Smith's Story click here!

ALSO BY KRIS MICHAELS

Hope City

HOPE CITY DUET - Brock and Sean

HOPE CITY - Brody- Book 3

Hope City - Ryker - Book 5

Kings of the Guardian Series

Jacob: Kings of the Guardian Book 1

Joseph: Kings of the Guardian Book 2

Adam: Kings of the Guardian Book 3

Jason: Kings of the Guardian Book 4

Jared: Kings of the Guardian Book 5

Jasmine: Kings of the Guardian Book 6

Chief: The Kings of Guardian Book 7

Jewell: Kings of the Guardian Book 8

Jade: Kings of the Guardian Book 9

Justin: Kings of the Guardian Book 10

Christmas with the Kings The Kings of Guardian

Drake: Kings of the Guardian Book 11

Dixon: Kings of the Guardian Book 12

Passages: The Kings of Guardian Book 13

Promises: The Kings of Guardian Book 14

A Backwater Blessing: A Kings of Guardian and Heart's Desire Crossover Novella

Montana Guardian: A Kings of Guardian Novella

Guardian Defenders Series

Gabriel

Maliki

John

Guardian Security Shadow World

Anubis (Guardian Shadow World Book 1)

Asp (Guardian Shadow World Book 2)

Lycos (Guardian Shadow World Book 3)

Thanatos (Guardian Shadow World Book 4)

Tempest (Guardian Shadow World Book 5)

Smoke (Guardian Shadow World Book 6)

STAND ALONE NOVELS

SEAL Forever - Silver SEALs

A Heart's Desire - Stand Alone

Hot SEAL, Single Malt (SEALs in Paradise)

Hot SEAL, Savannah Nights (SEALs in Paradise)

ABOUT THE AUTHOR

USA Today and Amazon Bestselling Author, Kris Michaels is the alter ego of a happily married wife and mother. She writes romance, usually with characters from military and law enforcement backgrounds.

Printed in Great Britain
by Amazon